Annie Carey

The History of a Book

Annie Carey

The History of a Book

ISBN/EAN: 9783337325879

Printed in Europe, USA, Canada, Australia, Japan

Cover: Foto ©Andreas Hilbeck / pixelio.de

More available books at **www.hansebooks.com**

THE

HISTORY OF A BOOK.

BY

ANNIE CAREY,

AUTHOR OF

"THREADS OF KNOWLEDGE," "AUTOBIOGRAPHY OF A LUMP OF COAL," ETC.

CASSELL, PETTER, & GALPIN,

LONDON, PARIS, AND NEW YORK.

PREFACE.

NOT more than 430 years ago a PRINTED BOOK, however dull and dry, was looked upon with respectful admiration, because it was regarded as a triumph of skill and ingenuity as wonderful as it was rare. Not so in these days. " What a stupid book!" is not unfrequently the verdict passed after a hasty glance of a few minutes, and the book thus denounced is immediately tossed down and deemed unworthy of further notice.

Yet never did a *printed* book stand forth more clearly as the sign and token of the world's progress in Science and Art—in all things requiring the clear head and the clever hand—than it does at the present time, be the author of it ever so stupid, and the subject-matter ever so dull and uninteresting.

The object of the present work is to call attention to this fact by describing some of the many and complicated processes involved in, and dependent upon, the ART OF PRINTING; and thus showing somewhat of the thought and skill, the care and labour, which are more or less required and expended whenever a Book is " Printed and Published."

A. C.

CONTENTS.

— ∗⋄∗ —

LIST OF ILLUSTRATIONS.

—⋄⋄—

The History of a Book.

INTRODUCTION.

In a dark, dingy room, forming the back part of an auctioneer's premises, stood an old gentleman, one dreary afternoon, studying most intently an ancient-looking volume. How long he might have remained thus standing, motionless and absorbed, under the one gas-light, had not a slim slip of a boy interrupted him, it is impossible to say.

"Guv'ner left his compliments," said the boy, holding out the gentleman's hat with one hand, and beginning to turn the gas down with the other; "and 'opes you'll 'ave a pleasant night in this uncommon pleasant 'ole of a place. Guv'ner's gone 'ome hisself, and I'm a-going to do the same—leastways, when I've put out this 'ere gas."

"Bless my soul!" exclaimed the old gentleman, who had not heard a word of the lad's saucy speech, but who perceived that the light was becoming less: "why, it's getting dark, I declare. I had no idea it was so late;" and, taking his hat from the boy, with a pleasant "good night," to which the lad replied civilly enough, he left the room.

The boy followed him, locked the door, put the key in his pocket, and the place was left to darkness and silence.

It was, of course, a trifle darker now that the gas was put out; but it could not well be more foggy and fusty, misty and musty, than it had been all that dreary November day.

During the preceding week several very old books, and two or three rare MSS., waifs and strays from the library of a learned and eccentric man, lately deceased, had been added to the many books already in that dingy room. These last arrivals lay on a common deal table, laden with dust—a state of things to which they were well accustomed, and which, therefore, did not in the least discompose them.

But lying, also, on this dusty table was a perfectly new book, which had been bought that very day by the old gentleman, as a present to his grandson, but which had been forgotten by him, and left behind.

This New Book felt, as was natural, exceedingly disgusted with the room and all that belonged to it, for only that afternoon had the New Book left, for the first time, the paternal publishing house. At his former home he had seen none but carefully-dressed companions, many of whom were also, like himself, handsomely ornamented, and all were fresh and clean and bright. There had always been plenty of life and activity around him; well-dressed ladies and gentlemen going in and out; smart young men to attend upon them, and upon himself and his associates. He had also, while there, been accustomed to be immensely admired and tenderly touched; and now to be thus neglected—left lying in dust and dirt and darkness, with no companions, save a set of disreputable old fogies —bah! it was altogether too bad.

Now, while the New Book was bemoaning his present condition, hating the place and despising his companions, the said companions were resenting his appearance among them as a great and unpardonable offence.

What business had youth and beauty, freshness and life, in their august company, with the dust of ages upon them, and the wisdom of the illustrious dead enshrined within them!

Presently a rustle and flutter, as of the wind among dry leaves, denoted that the feelings of the inhabitants of that room were going to find expression in some way or other. An old Law Book, whose yellow parchment coat was fastened together by two small pieces of cord and two little black buttons, and whose skin was shrivelled to an incredible degree, began to open out upon the subject. He evidently acted as clerk of the sessions.

"Pray, young sir," said the Law Book, "may I be so bold as to inquire by what title we ought to address you, and what are your birthplace and lineage; that we may be the better able to judge what are your claims and credentials for admittance into this most worshipful society of ancient Books and MSS.?"

"Possibly you may not be aware," said a dark, black, dry-looking Quarto, before the New Book could reply, "that every one who enters this our most ancient and learned guild is expected to be able to contribute to the edification of its members. We are accustomed to pass our nights in learned and profitable discourse, such as befits our age and character. Now, you are evidently so new to life, and (if you will excuse me), judging from your ornamented exterior, so frivolous, that I much fear you can have but scant store of thoughts and information to communicate."

"Very true indeed, very true," said a chorus of obscure Books in the background. "What can he have to say?—such a new book, such a dandy!"

"Then, also, we are accustomed to enliven our intercourse with relations of our past experiences, abroad and at home; of the many great men we have known during our long lives—men great and mighty in the world of letters, but who are only mere names to *you*, so fresh as you are from your paternal house."

"And some of us have passed our lives, or part of them, among crowned heads and titled dames," said a rare French MS., with a rich vellum dress, who, having been in past days a court beauty, was accustomed to expect and to receive a great deal of attention; "but you, I presume, gaily as you are dressed, have not yet been presented at court. You are so young; you can know nothing of life, and men and manners, of sages and courtiers, kings and queens, poets and painters, divines and senators!"

"Very true indeed!" echoed the chorus. "What can he know?—such a new book, such a beauty, such a dandy!"

Now, our New Book had entered the room with a very good opinion of himself, but he began now to feel rather small and ignorant, and, at the same time, he was somewhat ruffled at the disparaging remarks made about him. However, being possessed of a considerable amount of courage and love of adventure, he plucked up spirit, and replied:

"In answer to the first speaker, who inquired my name and lineage, I beg to say I am a native of London, and one of an ancient family. The title by which I am known is 'The Life and Adventures of Robinson Crusoe.'"

"You don't mean to say so!" exclaimed a dingy, brown Octavo. "Why, we are *brothers;* that is also my own name and title. Our common parent, Daniel Defoe, would be delighted if he could but know how much we are esteemed, and how widely we are spread abroad. He, Defoe, was born—as, doubtless, you know—in the year 1661; and of all his book-children (and he had many), there was none for which he had such love as for his 'Robinson Crusoe,' which he sent forth to the world 1719. Mankind, young and old, evidently agrees with him. You know that Dr. Johnson (you may have heard of him, though he lived between 1709 and 1784) once said that there were only three books which men wished to be longer than they were, and named 'Robinson Crusoe' as one of those three. I had no idea that any of us were so newly established in the world, and so well-to-do, as you apparently are. In my young days, I was considered to be beautifully got up—in fact, quite regardless of expense; though I do not remember that I ever wore purple and gold. But if you have the advantage over me somewhat in personal exterior, yet you will allow that my great age (I am 107 years old, and was the thirteenth edition of our family) makes me of more value than yourself. Still, I am delighted to see you."

Now, the New Book, it must be confessed, was not particularly overjoyed at meeting his old, sallow-complexioned, brown-coated relative. Truth to say, he trembled a little lest his own beautiful purple coat, with its gold embroideries, and his spotlessly white linen, should be soiled by the touch of the other. But he did not disgrace his bringing up, and the house from which he came, by showing his dislike.

Certainly, the difference between the two books, in every single respect—such as external binding, colour and texture of paper, ink, and letter-press—was as great as it could well be.

" I can well believe that Defoe Senior never resembled his relative, Defoe Junior, in dress and general appearance, even though their ages are not, after all, so far apart," remarked the French MS. to her neighbour, an English MS. of the fourteenth century. Both of the MSS., from their great age, superior refinement, and real historical value, looked with scorn upon the pretension of books of the eighteenth century, such as the Senior Defoe. [The Books were so accustomed to look upon themselves as part and parcel of their several authors, and to regard these authors as belonging to them (the Books) rather than the books to the authors, that they frequently went by the name of their authors or compilers.] The Senior Defoe was about to make some angry, and therefore, most likely, absurd reply, when a venerable, dust-becovered, weather-stained Folio, of the largest size, gave notice that he wished to speak. This Folio had a most weighty and imposing appearance, even though his yellow-brown sheep-skin coat hung in tatters about him. He was not quite so old as some of the books present, certainly not so old as the MSS., the year of his birth being 1563; but he was regarded as the father of the community, and was always listened to with great respect.

" It appears to me," said the Great Folio, " that the differences between Defoe the Senior and Defoe the Junior are so many and striking, as to show that mankind must have greatly altered the ways and means by which the present generation of books are brought up and brought out to the world—in other words, are printed and published. Possibly the world may have become wiser and better than we in our solitude are apt to imagine. At any rate, it would be interesting and profitable to hear somewhat of the new methods now employed, and to compare them with those with which we have been personally acquainted. Perhaps our young friend, who has so recently passed through the press, and in whom I am pleased to discern marks of good family and gentle breeding, would be so obliging as to tell us how these matters are now managed."

Our New Book, encouraged by the paternal tone of the Great Folio, replied at once, modestly and cheerfully : " I shall be very glad, venerable sir, to tell you and all the assembled company of the many different and wonderful processes through which I have passed in coming to my present state. As the ancient

Quarto wisely remarked, I am too young to be able to say anything to you that can be called ' edifying ; ' and it would be impertinent of me, in the presence of so much black-letter erudition, to attempt to sermonise."

" So much the better," murmured the French MS., who, being of a light and airy disposition, was apt to get weary under the twenty-eighth head of some of the divines.

" Neither have I personal recollections of great and distinguished men to relate to you. Any information I may possess of my great master, Defoe, derived from vague and shadowy memories of a former state of existence, will be far better communicated by my aged relative."

[The New Book was quick-witted, and had found out that in this Book Society the surest sign of wealth, and the best passport to distinction, was for a Book to possess " ages for its dower ; " and that to be called " venerable " was considered a complimentary mark of esteem. It is not always so in other societies.]

" But there is one thing I can do, and will do with pleasure, and that is to give you a true and faithful account of my education and bringing out—that is, the *History of a Modern Book*."

CHAPTER I.

HISTORY OF PRINTING.

"BEFORE our young friend begins his history," said the French MS., "I should much like to hear a little about the invention of this wonderful art of printing, of which you all make such a boast. You must excuse me if I confess that I do not clearly perceive the immense superiority of a BOOK over a MS. We, MSS., contain letters upon vellum or paper; *we* communicate instruction; and *we* are often, like yourselves, 'profusely illustrated.' (Is not that the right term?) Where, then, is the great difference between us?"

"I am quite sure that your ladyship's title to respect and consideration is one of the highest," replied the New Book; "yet——"

"Let me mention her ladyship's full title to you; I do not think you have yet heard it," said the Law Book, who then, in a somewhat dry, pompous manner, gave out this title, as if reading from a catalogue: "Premier Volume du Mireoir Historial. Translate de Latin en François, par Frère Jéhan de Vignay."

"Much obliged to you," said the New Book, coolly. "I was going to observe that, valuable as your ladyship undoubtedly is, both from the information you can communicate and your own great age, yet that, of necessity, your true worth can only be known to a very select few; to *copy* your excellences is, as none can know better than yourself, a labour involving great difficulty and much time—almost impossible to the rough and busy world of to-day. *You* are written by hand upon paper—I beg pardon, vellum; and in no other way can you be multiplied as a MS. But in *printing*—letter-press printing—the letters or marks are produced upon the paper by pressing the paper upon letters that have been cut out of wood, or *cast from moulds* of metal, so that *many impressions* of the same thing can be taken from the one set of letters; and as, now at least, these letters are separate and movable, the same letters can be rearranged and made to produce other and different books. These are, you must allow, great differences, and great advantages."

"The world was a long time in finding out this said wonderful art," remarked a MS. of the fourteenth century, written in Latin, but executed in England, and, therefore, known in that room as the English MS.

" It has always been a matter of great surprise to me," said the Great Folio, "that an invention apparently so simple should have been discovered so late; especially when one remembers how many things the ancients did that might have suggested the art. Look at the Chaldeans and the Egyptians carving their characters, their hieroglyphics, on bricks and stones, and taking impressions of seals and stamps upon wax and clay."

" And we know," said the Quarto, "that in old Homer's days they engraved maps upon metal; and friend Virgil tells us that the Romans used 'brands' or separate letters for marking cattle."

" But they never seem to have thought of putting ink, or some similar substance, upon these plates, and transferring the impression on to paper, or some substitute for that material," said the Great Folio. " Strange to be so near to, and yet so far from, the discovery."

" The Chinese seem to have come the nearest," remarked the Law Book; " for I have heard that they actually did transfer impressions—that is, *print* from characters on blocks—some say as early as 900 years before the Christian era. But, as every one knows, the Chinese always claim to be the first in discovering a thing, whatever it may be. However, the Chinese chronicles seriously affirm that, 50 B.C., the Chinese regularly printed books, first on silk, and afterwards on paper; and that date makes them nearly 500 years in advance of the rest of the world."

" How did they manage their printing?" inquired the English MS.

" Somewhat in the way they actually do now in some parts of China. Every

CHINESE RICE-PAPER PLANT, AND METHOD OF PREPARING THE PAPER.

B

page of the work intended to be printed is first carefully written on their transparent paper; the paper is then placed face downwards upon a block of wood, and the engraver cuts away all the parts of the wood where there are no marks, thus leaving the letters themselves standing up in relief upon the wood. The letters are then inked, the sheet of paper laid upon them, and pressed down by means of a brush. No printing-press is used. Of course, as many distinct blocks are needed as there are pages in the book, and the blocks can only do for that one particular kind of book," replied the Law Book.

" These whole blocks of letters remind me of our modern stereotyped plates," said the New Book. " It was certainly a great step towards regular printing; but one wonders they did not go a little further, and cut *separate letters*."

" I believe the Venetians brought the knowledge of this block-engraving into Europe; at any rate, it is certain that the first attempt at *printing* was by engravings, or letters cut on wood," said the Great Folio.

" And I remember when, at the end of the fourteenth century, playing-cards were invented for the amusement of his Majesty Charles VI. of France. I suppose they were made in some such way?" said the English MS.

" Yes; they were, it is said, the first things attempted," replied the Quarto, with a sharp click of his clasps; " but other and different things soon followed. Prints of figures, single or groups, for manuals of devotion. Block books with pictures, and a little explanation or description perhaps, engraved all on one block. Then came the idea of cutting out *single* letters; and thus began the grand art of printing."

" Permit me, for the honour of my country, to continue the narrative," interposed a very antiquated edition of Esop's Fables. " I was myself printed at Strasburg in the year 1556, and have been personally acquainted with some of the early results of this great invention. My own city, Strasburg, if it may not claim the honour of being the one from whence printed books were first issued to the world, yet was the one in which the great Gutenberg, the Father of Printing, first carried out his grand idea, that of making and printing from *movable metal types*."

" Excuse my interrupting, but I must beg to remind you and all assembled that Haerlem, in Holland, a city not far from my own birthplace, claims the honour of being the one from which a *printed book* first issued to the world; and in the great square of that city stands a bronze statue to Laurentius, or Laurens Coster—as some will call him—the man whom the Dutch regard as undoubtedly *the* inventor of the art of printing."

This speech proceeded from a Book which in that room went by the name of

EXAMPLES OF EARLY BLOCK-PRINTING.

" the Elzevir," because it came from the office of the renowned brothers, the Elzevirs, printers at Amsterdam and Leyden. Sometimes, by the lighter order of books, it was called " The Animadversions," its real title being " Animadversiones in Acta Apostolorum."

" I do not in the least wish to detract from the honour of Haerlem, or of Laurentius, as you seem to prefer to call him, though you must know he is generally spoken of as Coster (whether from its being his surname, or merely a name derived from the office held by his father, and subsequently by himself); but you are aware that the accounts given of the way in which he first conceived

B 2

THE BURNING BUSH.
FROM "THE POOR MAN'S BIBLE."
AN EXAMPLE OF EARLY BLOCK-PRINTING.

the idea of printing, and the way he carried out those ideas, are unsatisfactory and inconsistent, to say the least of it," retorted the Esop.

"Probably they may be, and are so. I do not mean to argue the point with you," returned the Elzevir. "All I wish to maintain is, that Laurentius, a wealthy and highly-respectable citizen and magistrate of Haerlem, did, before the year 1440, print and bring out certain books, printed from movable *wooden types.*"

"Perhaps so," retorted the Esop; "but you will allow that Coster *never* printed from METAL types, and that neither he nor his descendants ever brought the art to any great perfection. That was certainly effected in other lands, and by other men."

"Is it not probable that the chief principle in the art of printing was discovered by the two men in the two places pretty nearly about the same time, and without either being indebted to the other? In the course of my long life I have often observed that this has been the case with important discoveries and inventions, and then the honour may, with equal justice, be claimed alike by the contemporaneous discoverers. But pray oblige us with some account of your illustrious country-

ENLYMERODACH WITNESSING HIS FATHER BEING CUT INTO THREE HUNDRED PIECES.
FROM CAXTON'S "GAME OF YE CHESSE."

man John Gutenberg," said the Great Folio, who much feared a wordy combat between the Esop and the Elzevir, the representatives of the two nations.

"John Gutenberg," resumed the Esop, with recovered cheerfulness, "was born of noble family at Mentz, or Mayence, as it is now generally called. I believe the exact date of his birth cannot be fixed, but it was about the year 1400.

He settled at Strasburg in 1424, entered into partnership with some of its citizens, and promised to reveal to them certain secrets, which would not only serve to enrich themselves, but be of great value to the world. Unfortunately, Dritzehen, the citizen at whose house the work was carried on, soon died. On hearing of his death, Gutenberg sent his servant, Bieldich, to the brother of Dritzehen, with this message : ' Your late brother has four pieces lying beneath a press. John Gutenberg prays you to take them out and off the press, so that no one may see what it is.' But he was too late; the formes—*i.e.*, the fastened-together types—were already gone. The secret was discovered. Nicholas Dritzehen claimed to succeed to his brother's share, and a lawsuit followed, of no interest to us, except this—that it proved *beyond dispute* that Gutenberg had actually printed with *movable type*, the letters being *cut by hand*, either in metal or wood. Gutenberg left Strasburg, and went back to his native city, Mentz. There he laboured, and spent time and trouble, and all his own money, upon his loved pursuit. Becoming very poor, he prevailed on a wealthy goldsmith and worker in metals, one John Fust, or Faust, to join him, and the two set up *their* great printing firm. Doubtless the firm from which our young friend issued has a deservedly high and wide reputation, and many another firm besides ; but I question whether there has ever been, or will ever be, one that has earned such a world-wide celebrity as this of ' Gutenberg and Fust.' "

A murmur of assent was heard from all the assembly.

" How did Gutenberg make his letters ? " asked the English MS.

" He appears to have cut them all out by hand—at first, perhaps, in wood, but afterwards in *metal*," replied the Esop. " The first work supposed to be issued by the firm of Gutenberg and Fust was the copy of an indulgence granted by Pope Nicholas V. in 1451. Some copies of this are known bearing the date 1454." A grunt of dissatisfaction was heard from the Black-letter Quarto, which, as it was a translation of one of Calvin's works, 1573, need not be wondered at. The Esop proceeded : " In the archives of Mayence there was found an almanack for the year 1457, and which, therefore, must have been printed in the latter end of 1456. But during the years 1450 to 1455, Gutenberg brought out his grand work, The FIRST BIBLE. This Bible was all printed from separate metal types, *cut by* hand. Great was the wonder which the appearance of this work excited; for no one, except those who were actually concerned in its production, could imagine how it had been executed. Few could read it, unfortunately, for it was in Latin. It consisted of 637 leaves; some of the copies were on vellum, others on paper. Gutenberg must have been a man of taste as well as skill, and he evidently bestowed much loving care on this his great and chief work, for he ornamented all the letters commencing the different chapters. The initial letter of the first Psalm is, I understand, most beautiful. It is ornamented with foliage, flowers, a bird, and a greyhound, painted in a pale blue, with the ornamentation red."

"I heard, during the lifetime of our late owner, who well knew how to esteem an ancient book," said the Great Folio, "that a copy on vellum of this Bible sold, in 1825, for £504."

"Ah! but what do you think I heard only the other day?" exclaimed the New Book with some exultation. "That a copy on paper of this same Bible was sold for the sum of £2,690; while a copy on *vellum*, in the original binding, sold for the incredible sum of £3,400!"

Considerable excitement followed this announcement.

"Well done," exclaimed the Esop; "I am glad to find such power among men of estimating the great value of such a book. But who could have imagined that one of that first edition had survived all these years?"

"I have been told," said the New Book, "that there are about twenty copies in existence—not, of course, all perfect ones. The copy on paper that was sold the other day was, I heard, 'absolutely perfect, with the edges of the paper uncut and rough as they came from the press.' Really, it must be a magnificent specimen of printing; the paper so thick and good; the colour of the ink so bright and deep, and the 'impressions' so perfect and regular, that the *best* of our modern work cannot excel it, even with all the advantages we possess. And as to the poorer kind of work, it will never live half the time of this Gutenberg Bible."

"Was the copy on vellum equally perfect?" asked the English MS.

"No; two leaves had been supplied by fac-simile, but they are so admirably done that they can hardly be discovered," replied the New Book. "This copy, I understand, can be traced back to its home in the library of the Mentz University. I believe there are only six or seven copies on vellum to be found, and these are in different public libraries."

"What an honour to be on the same shelf with one so venerable and so great!" exclaimed the Great Folio; "would that the honour were mine. But our friend the Esop will kindly resume his interesting narrative."

"As you may imagine," continued the Esop, "the expense of bringing out such a work with metal types cut by hand was exceedingly great; so great, indeed, that John Fust became dissatisfied, dissolved partnership, and commenced a lawsuit against Gutenberg. Vexed, wearied, and altogether disheartened, my unhappy friend retired from business, entered the service of the Elector Adolphus of Nassau in 1465, and died about three years afterwards. Not the first, and, I dare say, not the last, of the world's benefactors who have died weary and nigh broken-hearted," said the Esop, with something very like a sigh.

"And was the printing firm wholly broken up?" inquired the English MS.

"By no means," replied the Esop. "When Fust dissolved partnership with Gutenberg, he took his apprentice Schœffer as partner, and the firm became Fust and Schœffer. In less than eighteen months they brought out their wonderful Psalter; but it must be remembered that this work had been in hand some three or four years, so that most undoubtedly Gutenberg must have had a great share in its production."

"I have heard that this Psalter was an exceedingly beautiful work," said the Great Folio.

"You may well say so," replied the Esop. "It was of folio size, printed on vellum, from *cut* metal types. The capital letters were all cut in wood; and the initial letters of each of the Psalms were executed in three colours—black, red, and blue."

"Why, they must have passed *three* times through the press," remarked the New Book. "Are there many or any copies of this Psalter now in existence, I wonder?"

"I believe only about six or seven, and each of these differs from the other in some respects, showing the individual care bestowed on each. The best copy is to be found in the Royal Library at Vienna. In this Psalter of Fust and Schœffer, the printer's name, date, and place of publication are marked; and it is the first instance on record of a practice which is now so common," said the Great Folio.

"Ah, I remember to have heard, not so long after I was myself printed, which was in 1634, that the copy of this famous Psalter now at Vienna had been brought from the castle of Ambras, near Inspruck, where it had been discovered in 1664," remarked the Elzevir.

"I wonder how the Psalter got into the *castle?*" said the French MS. "If you had said *convent*, I should not have been surprised."

"Well, books travelled about even in those early times; and some warriors and kings valued books sufficiently to make collections of them," replied the Elzevir. "Matthias Corvinus, elected King of Hungary 1464, managed, amid all his fighting for crown and kingdom, to gather together a right famous library, rich in stores of classical antiquity. I have heard that as many as thirty amanuenses had been employed in copying MSS., and illuminating them most splendidly. The wretched Turks destroyed many of these treasures when they took Buda. And from this same library, the Archduke Francis Sigismund carried away a great number of MSS. and books, to add to his own collection in the castle of Ambras."

"I do not know how the world looks upon people who carry away books or in any way injure or lose them," said the French MS.; "but I know the good monks in my day had a great horror of the book-stealer. In the inside of MSS. may be found warnings to this effect: 'This book belongs to ——,' mentioning the name of the convent; 'whoever shall steal it, or sell it, or in any way alienate it from the house, or mutilate it, let him be anathema—maranatha. Amen.' Or, 'Whosoever removes this volume from this convent, may the anger of the Lord overtake him in this world, and in the next, to all eternity. Amen.'"

"Our late owner would have been glad to have thus anathematised the persons who borrowed his books and never returned them. I know he lost a great many in that way," said the Virgil.

"It appears to me," remarked the Great Folio, "that the world is very much

indebted to all founders of large national libraries. Without them not a tenth
of the books that are now in existence could have been preserved. I crinkle all
over when I think of the wicked burning of the famous library at Alexandria.
A history of the principal libraries that have been and still are established, with
an account of their founders, and, if possible, of the means by which they accumulated treasures, would, it strikes me, be very interesting. Very likely some such
history may already be in existence. But I hinder our friend the Esop from
proceeding with his narrative."

"I was only going to remark," resumed the Esop, "that the young man
Schœffer was of an exceedingly ingenious turn of mind. To him belongs the
honour of first *casting type in a matrix.* He worked in private and made matrices
for all the letters of the alphabet; and when he had cast the letters from them,
he showed them to his partner Fust. He was delighted with the invention, and
gave Schœffer his daughter Christina for wife. The labours of Fust and Schœffer
were soon after this interrupted. The Elector Adolphus of Nassau laid siege
to Mentz in 1462, the printing firm was broken up, and the workmen dispersed.
Fust went to Paris, where he sold his books in such quantities, and at such
low prices, that people could not understand how it could be managed; and as
ignorant people generally dislike and fear what they cannot understand, so these
good people grew alarmed and a trifle malicious, and declared that the Evil One
must of a certainty have a hand in the matter. So the name of 'Dr. Faustus'
became associated with all kinds of queer black stories, and, I suppose, remains
so to this day."

"The siege of Mentz and the breaking up of the printing firm were good
things, after all; or, rather, good came of them," said the Quarto.

"Yes; for the workmen, being scattered, carried the knowledge of the art
away with them to other places," said the Esop. "Tours, Rome, Venice, Paris,
and Strasburg soon had printing-presses of their own. Indeed, in less than
fifteen years from the siege of Mentz, every southern European town of any note
had its press and printers."

"The art appears to have flourished greatly in Italy, for we soon hear of
new kinds of type being introduced. In 1467, Conrad Sweinheim and Arnold

Pannurtz, printers at Rome (the first was a German, by-the-by), brought in what is called the Roman type, and Greek and Hebrew characters were cast not long afterwards. Indeed, Italy has great reason to be proud, for at Milan, as early as 1476, the first Greek grammar was printed; and at Florence, in 1488, was published by one Demetrius, a native of Crete, a splendid folio edition of Homer's works," said the Elzevir.

" Pray, don't forget to mention," put in the Esop, "a quarto edition of an elder brother of mine, two years before the Homer."

" And a still greater triumph was achieved," continued the Elzevir, "for, in 1488, the books of the Old Testament were printed in Hebrew character, at a small town in the duchy of Milan. Then at Bâsle, in 1516, Erasmus printed his Greek Testament; and in 1518 the Venetian Septuagint was published."

" If the Evil One had a hand in this invention of printing, it was strange work for him to do; for almost all the works of the early printers were either for the healing of the body or the healing of the soul," remarked the Quarto.

" Excuse me, I pray you, one moment," said a Spanish Book, with grave, courtly politeness, though his coat was but of weather-stained parchment; "allow me in your courtesy to remark, that to our Cardinal Ximenes belongs the honour of bringing out the entire Bible as a whole in the ancient languages."

" True," replied the Elzevir. "And to the great Luther belongs the honour of giving, in 1539, the Bible to his countrymen in *their own tongue;* to Lefevre for doing the same for his fellow Frenchmen; and to Tyndale and his noble companions, Frith and Miles Coverdale, for conferring a like boon on England. Tyndale, as you are aware, printed his English New Testament at Antwerp—being forced to flee from England—and sent it across the sea to England in 1526; and in 1535 the whole Bible, the united work of Tyndale and Miles Coverdale, was allowed by your Henry VIII. to be read at certain times in churches. A permission, alas, soon afterwards recalled."

" I thought the great English nation would not be long behind their neighbours in this wonderful art of printing," said the French MS.

" No, indeed," replied the Great Folio, with dignity. "So closely did the English follow, that they can scarcely be said to be *behind.* Towards the end of the reign of our Henry VI., the then Archbishop of Canterbury moved the king to send men to Haerlem to procure a 'printing mould' to be brought to this country! The king was pleased to consent, and appointed his master of the robes to manage the affair. It cost the king a great deal of money, and his

COVERDALE.

negotiators a great deal of trouble, for the people of Haerlem wished to keep the invention to themselves.

"Eventually, a workman of the name of Corsellis consented to come over. He was smuggled out of Holland in disguise, brought safe to London, carried with a guard to Oxford, and constantly watched till he had made good his promise to teach the English how to print. About the time of the Restoration, a book was discovered with this title, 'Expositio Sancti Jeronimi in Symbolum,' published at Oxford in 1468. So says Mr. Richard Atkins, who, in 1664, wrote a book about the 'Origin and Growth of the Invention of Printing.' Other presses were soon set up, at St. Albans, and at Westminster."

TYNDALE.

"But, indeed," exclaimed the New Book, somewhat hastily, "I have always heard that William Caxton was the *very* first who ever set up a printing-press in England; and excuse me, but every child now learns that that press was set up at *Westminster*, and not till 1474."

"Gently, my young friend; I do not speak without good reason," said the Great Folio, quietly. "I have not the least wish to rob Mr. William Caxton

—for whom I have immense esteem—of any of the honour rightly due to him. Unquestionably he was the *first* to print in England from movable *moulded metal* types. Corsellis seems to have only used wooden ones; the only kind, I believe, to which he had been accustomed at Haerlem."

" Truly," said the Quarto, " Mr. William Caxton was a most modest, upright, honourable man ; one worthy to be held in the highest estimation, for that he was ever anxiously desirous of the good of the nation. Kings and great men delighted to honour him, and supported him in all his undertakings. He was a native of London, and apprenticed to a mercer, one Mr. Robert Large, who, on his death, left him a considerable legacy. Mr. Caxton resided abroad for thirty years, and travelled about a great deal. When in Flanders, he was so much esteemed that he was employed by King Edward IV., with the title of ' Ambassador ' accorded to him, to negotiate a commercial treaty with the Duke of Burgundy, to whom Flanders then belonged. It was while he was in Flanders that he made himself practically acquainted with the art of printing, then in its infancy. He induced one of the workmen who had been obliged to flee from Mentz to join him, and they set up a press at Cologne. There he published a book called ' The Siege of Troy.' This book, he explains to his readers, was *printed,* ' not written with penne and inke as other bokes ben, to th ende that every man may have them at tone (at once), ffor all the books of this story, named the " Recule of the Historyes of Troyes," thus are prynted as ye here see, were begonne in oon day and also fynished in oon day.' In 1471, Caxton came to England, accompanied by two or three workmen, one of whom was the celebrated Wynken de Worde ; and set up his press in a small chapel adjoining West-minster Church. In our days a printer's office used to be called a ' chapel,' owing to the fact, I suppose, of the first office being in a chapel."

" The same term is still in use among printers," said the New Book ; " and I have heard that when the men have a meeting to frame or alter any laws they are said to ' hold a chapel.' "

" The English soon excelled in the art, according to Mr. Richard Atkins, who says, ' In the reigns of Edward IV., Richard III., Henry VII., and Henry VIII., the English proved so good proficients in printing, and printers grew so numerous, as to furnish the kingdom with books, and so skilful as to print them as well as any beyond the seas,'" said the Great Folio, with evident pride and pleasure; "and in my day printing was reckoned among the liberal arts; compositors were men often of gentle birth, and Doctors of Learning were 'readers for the press.' Sometimes the name of the corrector was put in the title-

WILLIAM CAXTON'S PRINTING-OFFICE IN WESTMINSTER ABBEY.

page, together with that of the printer, and an edition would be valued according to the name of the corrector."

"I cannot say our modern compositors and correctors, or, as we call them, 'readers for the press,' belong to the aristocracy either of birth or of letters," said the New Book; "yet you would find that they are clever, sensible men, with a fair proportion of education; and that 'the readers' certainly require and possess a great deal of varied knowledge. But please to continue your account of Mr. Caxton."

"The first book he printed in England was finished in March, 1474," continued the Quarto. "The title of this work was 'Ye Game and Playe of ye Chesse.'"

"Rather a strange book for a man like Mr. Caxton to choose as his first attempt in England—was it not?" said the New Book.

"Perhaps you are not aware," replied the Quarto, "that 'Ye Game of ye Chesse' is a collection of sixteen sermons, composed and delivered, in the first instance, for the edification of a particular king, who ——"

"O poor king! *sixteen* sermons expressly for himself; I am sorry for him! What had he done to be so punished?" exclaimed the French MS., *sotto voce.*

"Your ladyship's pity is thrown away in this case," replied the Black Quarto, grimly; "for the sermons were interspersed with *tales;* to suit them the better, I suppose, to the weak mental constitution of the royal listener."

"But what had the sermons to do with *chess?*" inquired the New Book.

"The game of chess was invented by a clever courtier, to show his master, the king, that there was a better way of amusing himself than by having his relatives hewn in pieces, or hanging up his prime ministers, one after another, as may be seen by the frontispiece * this king was in the habit of doing. The king listened to the sixteen sermons, learnt 'Ye Game of ye Chesse,' and became a better man from that time henceforward. And the book is written in order to show the good effects of learning to play chess, and to cultivate virtues, and recommends to 'every man that redyth or heerith this little book redde,' to 'take thereby ensample, to amende hym.'"

"You must excuse me," said the Virgil, "but you are doubtless aware that the game of chess was really invented by Pălămēdes, during the siege of Troy, 'to beguile of tedium of slaying Trojans, or waiting for them to come out and be slain.' I only mention the fact, as it is as well to give the honour, be it great or small, to the right person."

"I ask your excuse," replied the Quarto; "but my king, for whose moral benefit the game was expressly invented, lived a long time *before* that celebrated siege of Troy, so, of course, *that* settles the question as to who invented the game. But to return to the labours of Mr. Caxton. Between the years 1471 and 1491,

* See Illustration on page 21.

he had printed nearly seventy works—a very great number, considering how young the art was in those days."

" Was Caxton ever styled ' King's Printer?' " inquired the Senior Defoe.

" No, never," replied the Quarto, " though he printed largely for both Edward IV. and Henry VII. That title and office were not instituted till about 1500, and Mr. Caxton died 1494, pursuing his labours, through much infirmity, to the very last. One of the workmen who came over with him, Mr. Richard Pynson, was the first appointed by letters patent to that office. Wynken de Worde, another of his workmen, became very justly celebrated as one of the best printers in England. His ' black letter' was always greatly admired, and he was the first to introduce into England the Roman type. Wynken de Worde received the title, or gave it to himself, of ' Printer to the Lady Margaret, mother of King Henry VII.' This Lady Margaret must have been a clever woman, for she translated the fourth book of Thomas à Kempis's ' Imitation of the Life of Christ,' and Richard Pynson printed it by her commandment."

" Most of the early printed books, in England as well as abroad, seem to be either on divinity or physic," said the New Book.

" True, they were so," replied the Great Folio. " Learning was certainly not quite so varied in those days as it seems to be now."

" And law books were absolutely forbidden, I have understood," said the English MS., with a comical glance at the Law Book of the room.

" Perhaps—nay, I admit they were so, just at first," replied the Law Book ; " but Queen Elizabeth, the very first year of her reign, granted, by patent, ' the privilege of sole printing all books that touch or concern the common laws of England ' to Tottel, one of her servants, who ' kept it entire till his death.' And other royal personages followed her good example."

The Law Book appeared to think the shield of royal protection and patronage must be rather awe-inspiring, for he delivered his remarks with a solemnity befitting the wig and the woolsack.

" I believe the noble art of printing did not continue to advance in England at the same rate as during the first few years after its introduction—did it?" said the Elzevir.

C

"No," replied the Great Folio, sadly. "Many things hindered. Ignorance, superstition, cruel persecution for religious opinions—the excitement and heat of political passions during the time of the civil wars of Charles I., were all so many obstacles in the way of the nation's progress in literature. Yet the desire for intelligence, or, perhaps I ought to say, for 'news,' during the time of the wars was great, and led to the establishment of newspapers—first weekly, then twice or thrice a week. After the Revolution, 1688, printing greatly revived, and has gone on, I suppose, with increasing power and energy ever since. Between 1700 and 1756, I have heard that about 6,000 volumes were published. That seems to me an immense number; perhaps our young friend may think differently. But it is quite time we made way for that narration of his early history which he has kindly promised to give us, and which I beg he will now commence."

CHAPTER II.

THE ART OF PRINTING.

WITHOUT any attempt at a preface, the New Book began :—

"My first remembrances of myself date from a certain stage in my MS. life—an unsubstantial, loose, unbound condition of existence, in which I displayed by no means so bookish an appearance as the MSS. of the present company; for I was merely fastened together by a clip at one corner; neither did I possess the smallest trace of ornamentation, unless an occasional blot may be so called. I was leaning upon the left-hand side of the lower of two long shallow wooden trays. Both the upper and lower trays, or cases, were divided into compartments. These compartments contained letters, or types, as the printer styles them. In the upper case were arranged all the capitals, small capitals, accented letters, figures, and also the marks used by which to refer to notes. The divisions in this upper case, I perceived, were all of equal size; while those in the lower were unequal, showing that there were more letters in some than in others. The letter 'e' had the largest place of all. In this lower case there were the small letters, stops, and the blank spaces to put between the different words. I noticed that there were in the same room several 'frames,' many of them *double*, so that two men could stand at them, and containing numerous 'cases' of different 'founts' of type.

"In front of me stood an intelligent-looking man, in shirt sleeves and linen apron. But before I proceed to describe, for the sake of those of our company who may never have been in a 'composing-room,' the use this man made of me and of these letters, I may, perhaps, be allowed to say a word or two about the letters themselves.

"Each of the several kinds of letters, marks, stops, and other characters

á	é	í	ó	ú	§	‡	A	B	C	D	E	F	G
à	è	ì	ò	ù	‖	†	H	I	K	L	M	N	O
â	ê	î	ô	û	¶	•	P	Q	R	S	T	V	W
X	Y	Z	Æ	Œ	U	J	x	y	z	æ	œ	u	j
1	2	3	4	5	6	7	A	B	C	D	E	F	G
8	9	0	£	—	⌢	ñ	H	I	K	L	M	N	O
ã	õ	ỹ	ð	ũ	ç	k	P	Q	R	S	T	V	W

Upper Case.

—	[	æ	œ	(	j		thin spaces	'	þ	!	;	...	fl
& ffi	b	c	d	e			i	s	f	g	...	ff
ffi hair & spaces	l	m	n	h		o	y	p	,	w	em quads	...	ft
z x	v	u	t	thick spaces		ñ	r	q : . -			Large quads

Lower Case.

DIAGRAM SHOWING HOW TYPES ARE ARRANGED IN THE "CASES."

had required three things in order to make it—a punch or die, a matrix, and a type-mould. A letter had been first cut out in relief, the reverse way, upon the end of a piece of hardened steel, which is called the 'punch or die.' The raised letter had been struck into a piece of copper an inch and a half long, and wide in proportion to the required letter. A *sunken* impression of the raised letter on the die had thus been made. This piece of copper with the impression sunk in it is the 'matrix.' Now, if melted metal were poured into this matrix, there would, of course, be a raised copy made of the letter cut in the die.

DOUBLE FRAME.

"But that would not be sufficient to make what is strictly speaking a 'type.' The letter must have a body to it of a certain height and width. So the matrix had to be placed in what is called a 'type-mould.' This type-mould is made of steel, with an outer covering of wood. It is formed in two distinct parts, and the parts fit into and slide over each other, so that while the height remains the same for every kind of letter, the width can be altered, and the same mould serve for different kinds of type.

"The matrix was put in at the bottom of the type-mould. A man standing by the side of a furnace took up a little melted metal in a very small ladle, poured it in at the top of the mould, gave the mould a shake and a flourish over his head, in order to get the metal into all the crevices of the matrix; then touched a spring, separated the parts of the mould, and picked out the letter from the matrix and mould; and all this he did so quickly that, being a good caster, he could make about 500 letters an hour, or eight letters a minute. I ought to tell you that in the body part of each of the letters there was a good-sized *notch*, the use of which you will soon learn."

"I wonder what my transcriber and translator, Frère Jéhan de Vignay, would think of such quick movements. He could not cast his letters from the pen to the page much faster than that," said the French MS.

"A boy took the letters as they were thus cast," resumed the New Book, "nipped off the piece at the end of the metal that was not wanted, and took them to a man who rubbed them on a gritty stone, to remove any little knobs or globules of metal. From him they went to another man, the 'dresser,' who polished them on each side, and planed the bottom and made a groove in it, so that each should stand perfectly even. They were then carefully examined by a magnifying glass, to see that they were all perfectly regular. All type must be of exactly the *same height*, and that is an inch; and all the letters belonging to any particular class of type must be of the same *thickness*, though the width may vary. So you may see that casting type from metallic moulds is a difficult and delicate work. All honour to the young man Schœffer, who first conceived the idea."

"It is certainly a much quicker way of making letters than cutting them out by hand, as Gutenberg seems to have done," said the Virgil.

"Indeed it is; and I ought to tell you that machines are now used for casting type, and that one of these can do the work of six men.

"The type was then assorted—that is, a certain number of each letter, more of some than of others, were counted out, together with the spaces, &c., and each bundle of letters tied up in lengths. A complete set of letters thus assorted is called a 'fount.'"

"I suppose there are many different sizes of type? It was so, I know, in my day," said the Elzevir.

"There are as many as twenty or thirty different sizes I believe," replied the New Book; "but only about twelve of these are used for book-work. Their names and appearances, in order of size, are :—

## Great Primer. ## English. ## Pica.	Small Pica. Long Primer. Bourgeois. Brevier.	Minion. Nonpareil. Pearl. Brilliant.

"Brilliant is the smallest type made. I am, myself, printed in long primer."

"Ah, those old names," said the Great Folio, "recall the old days when the different types received different names, according to the different prayers of the Romish Church for which they were employed. Thus the type used for printing the 'Primarius,' or 'Prayers for the Virgin,' was called *primer*; that employed for the 'Breviary,' or 'Book of Daily Prayer,' *brevier* type; while that which was used for printing the 'Service of the Mass' was called *pica*—and so termed because of the glaring contrast of the black and white on the page. Strange to see how facts get handed down in mere names."

"There is one question I should like to ask," said a thin, sallow treatise on "The Mysteries of Nature," known generally by the name of "the Mystery," and who was not popular. "And that question relates to the nature of the metal that is melted and used for the purpose of forming these types. Printers, I know, formerly used a mixture of lead and a metal they spoke of as 'regulus,' though its real name was antimony; known to the ancients, according to Pliny, by the name of stibium."

"And printers still use that term 'regulus,'" said the New Book; "and they use the same metals in the proportion of ——"

"That term 'regulus,' or 'the little king,' I was about to observe," continued the Mystery, in a thin dry voice, "was given to the metal antimony on account of the mysterious way in which it controlled the other metals, especially gold, altering their dispositions, and making them act contrariwise to their usual methods. This metal regulus hath a strange power. Then it is highly poisonous, and not fit for use by ignorant people. The Parliament of France, in 1566, forbade its use altogether; and, in 1608, its use was restricted to the Faculty—a wise and wholesome regulation."

"Yes, perhaps," said the Esop, "if people are no wiser now than was poor Basil Valentine, its modern discoverer, in the sixteenth century. He, you know, with the best intentions, gave his brother monks, in the convent at Erfurth, the same strength of dose which he had given to the hogs belonging to the monastery. The hogs grew fat—the poor monks died. As the medicine was considered to have a special dislike to the monks, it was called 'antimony—antimoine.' Pray, have people found out at length in what way to use it as a medicine?"

"O dear, yes," replied the New Book. "In proper quantities, it is in great request, and found to be a most useful remedy.

"It is employed in the composition of type-metal in the proportion, generally, of one part antimony to four of lead. The antimony renders the lead harder, and the lead renders the antimony softer. Thus, in the alloy, that is, mixture of the two metals, the properties of each become somewhat modified. Now let us return to the composing-room, and leave the type-foundry."

"In my time printers were accustomed to cast their own types; you speak as if it were a separate business," said the Quarto.

"Don't you remember," said the Law Book, "that, in 1637, the art of type-founding was, by an edict of the Star Chamber, separated from that of printing, and that four founders were appointed; and these four for some time kept all the work to themselves? I suppose there are more type-founders in these times?"

"Certainly no such absurd laws now limit the manufacture," replied the New Book; "but the trade is still confined to a few firms."

"I was printed with the beautiful black-letter type of Wynken de Worde," said the Quarto, with a justifiable pride in his admirable letter.

"Wynken de Worde did a great deal, I know, in improving the type, and used to supply the printers of his day; but after his death, most of the type used in England came from Holland I believe," said the Elzevir.

"But I was printed with type from the foundry of one Mr. William Caslon, of London," said the Senior Defoe. "Caslon's type was considered so good that it used to be sent to other countries; and I have heard that, from 1720, or thereabouts, till 1780, there were few books in which his excellent type was not used."

"I believe it is allowed that the type manufactured in Great Britain is superior to all other; still I would not like to be positive on this point," said the New Book, courteously. "Let us return to the composing-room. I noticed that the man who stood in front of me held in his left hand what he called a 'composing-stick,' which was a hollow piece of iron with a slide in it, to move up and down at his pleasure. Giving a rapid but keen glance at me ('copy' he called me in

COMPOSING-STICK.

what I considered a rather disrespectful manner), he began to select letters from the cases before him. Taking up first the capital letter from the 'upper case' which corresponded to the first one on my page, he placed that in the left-hand lower corner of his composing-stick. The notch made in the front part of the body of the type enabled the man to tell, without looking at the letter, which was the right way to place it. The letter was placed with the top of it *next* to the man, and the *notch outwards*, turned away from him. Then his hand went to the 'lower case,' and he took out the necessary small letters and put them in one after another into the stick. The first word finished, the compositor put in a blank piece of metal, called a 'space.' All the spaces are shorter than the letters, so that the ink will not touch them when it is put upon the type. Thus he went on till he reached the end of the line. But then there came a difficulty. You see the words and the spaces must *exactly fill the line*, without being too tight or too loose. And the letters of a word cannot be allowed to run down the margin in the way that some ladies let their words go. And words, as you all know, can only be divided in certain ways. So my compositor had to take out some of the spaces and put thicker, wider ones in,—the spaces are of different widths,—taking great care, at the same time, that the spaces were evenly arranged. He could measure well with his eye, and very seldom required to make any alterations; but some men, I noticed, seemed to have a great deal of trouble in contriving and filling their lines. This arranging of words and spaces, and making the lines of proper length, is called 'justification.'"

"A strange misuse of the term," muttered the Quarto between his boards.

"The line finished, the compositor put a thin slip of metal in front of it, called a 'setting-rule.' This rule forced all the letters to keep in a straight tight line. Now I am called, technically speaking, 'thick-leaded'—not *thick-headed*, I beg to observe; but, if you notice, you will see there is more space between my lines than just the depth of the type alone would have made. So, to make this space, a piece of flat metal, called a 'lead,' was laid all along the line. These leads are only as high as the spaces, and always bear a certain proportion to the depth of the type; not of mine though, for, as I told you, my type is long primer; but of pica, that being used as a standard."

"That space between your lines is what makes your page look lighter and whiter than mine does, I suspect," said the Senior Defoe.

"That, together with other things," replied the New Book. "When the first line and the lead were arranged, the next was set up in the same way, letter by letter, space after space, till a dozen were thus composed.

"The stick being now full, and the setting-rule in front of the last line, the compositor most cleverly grasped the whole mass of type, with the aid of the setting-rule, and lifted it out of the composing-stick, and placed it, just as if it had been a solid bit, instead of a number of separate pieces, upon a tray, called a 'galley.' Then he went on again 'composing,' till stickful after stickful was placed on this galley. Most quickly and cleverly he did it all. But I saw an apprentice lad, who had taken a long time to fill his stick, drop the whole 'handful' upon the ground, just as he was going to place it on the galley. A handful of broken type is termed 'pye;' and the men laughed at him as he gathered up his spilt work, his pye; but I confess I felt sorry for the lad."

"Well, it was all in his day's work, I suppose," said the Law Book.

"But, you must remember, time is money, and a compositor is paid at a certain rate for every thousand letters composed," replied the New Book.

"The next thing my compositor did, when he had composed and put as much matter as he thought proper upon the galley, was to make it up into pages. He counted up the proper number of lines that were to make one page, and added at the bottom a line of 'quadrats.'"

"Pray, what are they?" inquired the English MS. "I must say your terms are peculiar, to say the least."

"Quadrats are, like the spaces, pieces of blank metal, but larger; sometimes they are three, four, five, or six times as long as they are broad; they form the blanks you see at the end of a paragraph. At the top of the page he put the folio, that is, the number of the page, and the title, and added some leads. At the foot of the first page he put a 'signature,' which, as you will

A CHASE.

afterwards find, is of great use in gathering and folding the printed sheets. Each page was tied up with strong string, or 'page-cord,' and laid upon an iron table. The next thing was to arrange a 'sheet' of these pages. As I am an 'octavo,' it required sixteen of my large pages to be made up and placed in order. The placing, or 'imposing,' the pages upon the large iron or stone table, called the 'imposing-stone,' is rather a difficult business, and one that requires practice to do it correctly and quickly. The pages have to be placed on the imposing-stone exactly the reverse way to that which they occupy in the sheet. For instance, my first page on the right hand (page of the book itself, I mean, not the Preface) was placed on the extreme left of the imposing-stone. When the pages required for one side of the sheet were placed, or ' imposed,' in the necessary order, the compositor took an iron frame, called a 'chase,' and laid it over the pages of type. This frame was divided by cross bars into compartments, and the man made the type secure to the frame, and the pages to each other, by means of various wedge-shaped pieces of metal and wood, termed ' furniture.' The whole mass of type, when thus securely ' locked together,' is called a ' forme.' Now, as both sides of a sheet of a book are printed, there must be two sets of arranged pages, or formes. One is called the ' outer forme,' and contains the first page on the right hand of the book, and all the other pages which, when the sheet is folded, will fall into their proper places. The other, the ' inner forme,' holds the second or left-hand page of the book, and all the rest of the pages which fall into their right places when the sheet is folded and cut open."

"It must be exceedingly difficult to know what pages to place on these two formes. It is a pity the pages cannot go in the straightforward way on the ' stone' that they do in the book itself," said the English MS.

"Like many other things, it becomes easy enough by habit and practice," replied the New Book. "Then, fortunately, there is a little fact which serves as a ready-made rule and guide. It is this—that the number on those pages which lie side by side on either of the formes will, when added together, make *one more than the number of pages* contained by the sheet. Take, for instance, the folio sheet, which has two leaves—that is, four pages. Well, on the outer forme the numbers on the pages are 1 and 4; those on the inner forme, 3 and 2; each pair of numbers making five, one more than the number of pages in the sheet. Take a sheet of quarto, which has four leaves = eight pages. The pages which stand side by side in the outer forme are 1 and 8, and 5 and 4—each pair making 9. In the inner forme there must be pages—$7 + 2 = 9$, and $6 + 3 = 9$. Take one more instance—my own sheet, which has sixteen pages. My outer forme held eight pages; arranged in couples, the numbers on these pages were : $1 + 16 = 17$, $13 + 4 = 17$, $8 + 9 = 17$, $12 + 5 = 17$. My inner forme held Nos. $3 + 14 = 17$, $15 + 2 = 17$, $6 + 11 = 17$, $10 + 7 = 17$. Each pair of numbers making, you see, one more than the number of pages in the sheet."

"What a most convenient thing," said the Æsop; "but how strange that it should so happen."

"Yes, it is curious, but it is true," said the New Book. "Now the formes, both outer and inner, being ready, a pressman inks the type, and, by means of a press kept for the purpose, a proof is 'pulled,' or taken, on common, I may say very common, paper, quite different to that which was used when I fairly 'went to press.' Sometimes, as I ought to have told you, the first proof is taken while the type is still on the galley, with a particular kind of hand-press kept for the purpose, and called a 'galley-press.' The proof was taken to the 'reader,' or corrector of the press. He carefully examined it to see that all was right as to

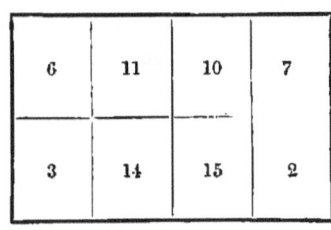

Outer Forme.   Inner Forme.

"IMPOSITION" OF A SHEET OF SIXTEEN PAGES.

the signatures, the folios—that is, numbers of the pages—the titles, spacing, and kind of type used, that no letter out of a different fount had got in by mistake. He also looked to see that the capitals, and the Italic letters, and the pointing were as the author intended them. The compositor then unlocked the formes, lifted out each line by the aid of a blunt bodkin that required to be altered, took out the wrong letter or letters, and put in the right ones. Then a fresh proof was taken, and sent to the author for correction. Now you can easily imagine that these corrections may often cause a great deal of trouble. A single letter can, of course, be altered without much difficulty; but a word added or taken away may require the moving of many lines, while the insertion of a sentence may oblige the compositor to 'overrun,' or re-arrange, a considerable number of paragraphs, or even pages.

"'Words is curus,' according to Aunt Chloe, and 'one word 'most as good as anodder;' but authors do not always agree with her, and object, naturally, to one word being changed for another, even when they are as much alike as 'Macedon and Monmouth.' But still they ought to remember the labour required by alterations, and make their writing as clear as possible, that the corrections may be as few as possible. It is reckoned, I believe, that it takes half as much time to 'overrun' as it does to 'set up the type' in the first instance. Another corrected proof, called a 'revise,' was then sent to the author, and afterwards again carefully read over by the 'reader for the press.' I cannot declare for certain that these readers were Doctors of Laws or Logic, or even of Divinity, as we have been told the 'correctors of the press used to be in the days of yore;' still, I do know that they were clever, educated men—and so also, to some extent, were the compositors. Speaking of compositors, reminds me that in the composing-rooms of some of our modern printing-offices, I could introduce you to a class of compositors which would, I suspect, be a novelty to all of you. I could show you '*women compositors.*'"

"Ah, indeed! To see women handling the composing-stick would be a strange and unexpected sight to all of us. There must be many a handful of 'pye,' I should imagine, on the floor of the rooms where *they* are employed. May I ask, pray, how long it is since women aspired to the office of compositors?" said the Esop, with a spice of scorn.

"The honour of having been the foremost one among the first to open the door for women to enter into this department of work belongs to Miss Emily Faithfull," replied the New Book, unmoved by the sneer of the Esop. "That lady, in early life, was greatly struck by the fact, that there are so few means of obtaining a livelihood open to women, and yet that there are such numbers of women who are obliged to work for their living. In 1860, Miss Faithfull set up a typographical establishment in London, and determined to ascertain, by careful trial, whether or not women were *able to set up type*. The experiment fully succeeded, difficulties and prejudices notwithstanding. 'The Victoria Press,' with its band of women workers, became a reality of common life; and Miss Faithfull was appointed 'Printer and Publisher in Ordinary to her Majesty.'

The business once fairly established, it passed into the hands of Miss Faithfull's manager; thus leaving her more at liberty to carry out her labours in other parts of the wide field of womanly interest and sympathy."

"And are women ever employed in this kind of work in other offices besides this said 'Victoria Press?'" inquired the Elzevir.

"O yes," replied the New Book. "Several offices in London, Edinburgh, Manchester, and elsewhere, taking courage from Miss Faithfull's success, now admit women as compositors. In the United States of America, Miss Faithfull says that women compositors are quite common. She herself, she tells us in some of her pleasant letters from America, published in the *Victoria Magazine,* visited Messrs. Harper's celebrated printing-office in Franklin Square, New York ; and the 'Riverside Press,' Boston ; and in both these places she not only found a large number of women employed as compositors, but had also the great pleasure of hearing the most unqualified testimony as to the real suitability of women for this work, their power of steady application to duty, and also of the good and pleasant influence exercised in many ways by their presence in the offices. But, perhaps, I ought to beg pardon for having introduced the subject."

"By no means," replied the Great Folio. "Of course, it appears very strange to us ; but I dare say the world may have altered in many of its ways and ideas since our young days."

"Well, it seems to me that, what with your 'compositors' and 'readers for the press,' and your 'proofs' and your 'revises,' and one thing and another, it takes a very great deal of trouble to make a *printed* book say what it means to say correctly. How much easier it is to draw the pen through a wrong word, as can be done in the case of a MS., and there's an end of the correction. But I confess it would have broken the heart of my Frère Jéhan de Vignay, if he had made many mistakes, and disfigured my pages with alterations and corrections," said the French MS.

"I know the old monks took great pains with their work, and that it was to many of them a real labour of love," said the Great Folio. "I am afraid our young friend would have considered some of the works that were issued in the days that followed the first establishment of printing to have been very carelessly turned out. In the first place, the words were often so close together that they were difficult to read; and as to the spelling, I fear it would have driven your correct ' readers ' crazy, it was so without rule and method. Then there were only two kinds of stops—the colon, and the full point. The leaves had no running title, and the pages no numbers. There were no capitals for the proper names and the beginning of sentences, and not unfrequently you will find the first word of a chapter without its initial letter."

"Excuse me," said the New Book, "but the Esop mentioned the capital letters both in Gutenberg's Bible and the Psalter of Fust and Schœffer."

"That is quite correct," replied the Great Folio. "The ornaments to the capital letters were, *at first*, extremely beautiful and costly; but as printing made progress, the art of ornamentation declined; and so it came to pass that the blanks left in the page for the initial letter to be put in by the hand of the ornamentist remained as they were left by the printer, and the word often went without its capital altogether. Then the printers in those days used many abbreviations, and these at last became so numerous as to need a book of explanations. The sizes of the books were also mostly cumbersome, like myself-- large folios or quartos."

"It was to lessen the number of the abbreviations that Aldus, a native of Rome, who set up a printing-press in Venice, invented, in 1696, the letter called after him, the Aldine, or *Cursious*. I think you call that letter in England by the name of ' Italic ;' is it still used ?" inquired the Esop.

"O dear, yes, very frequently," replied the New Book. "I ought to have mentioned that the Italic type is kept in a case underneath the lower part of the compositor's desk, or frame."

"This Aldus ought to be remembered," said the Elzevir, "for the great improvement he made in the Greek characters of those days. He, at any rate, was as particular about exactness as any one could wish ; for it is said that he ' considered it to be his duty to overlook *every sheet himself;* and that he declared he was so pressed with work as not to have time to eat or drink, or even to blow his nose.' The Aldine editions used to be famous for their correctness."

"Poor man," said the New Book; "why, he was as badly off as a modern editor.

" An editor! what's that?" inquired the French MS.

"'An editor," replied the New Book, with becoming gravity, "is a person who knows something of everything, and whose special business it is to find out the mistakes made by other people."

" What a *fearful* person!" exclaimed the French MS.

" By no means necessarily so," replied the New Book. " Of course, there are editors *and* editors ; but some editors, I can assure you, 'carry all their weight of learning' so lightly and easily that, really, you would not know them from ordinary people in good society."

" But as it is the duty of an editor to ' cut-up,' why, the sharper his knife is, the better for the purpose," said the Quarto.

" Perhaps so. An editor can be critical and crusty; and, I speak from personal knowledge, an editor can be critical and *courteous*, and yet the ' cutting-up' can be done equally well. When they are so, I know that some authors look upon editors as a delightful institution, and declare that they can sleep all the more soundly from knowing that there is some one in the world whose special mission it is to ' cut them up'—pleasantly, of course,—and to take care that they do not write nonsense.

" To return to my ' formes.' Just in the same way that the outer and inner formes of my first sheet were ' composed' and ' imposed,' and the proofs read and corrected, and re-read and re-corrected, so were the formes for all the other sheets belonging to me as a book. But before I take you to the Pressroom, there are several things that we ought to notice.

" In some cases, and for some purposes—such as newspaper and magazine printing, books that are published in parts, or books that are likely to be wanted in many editions—the pages of type, before they are carried to the press, or instead of being carried to the press, are ' stereotyped;' that is to say, a perfect *fac-simile* of the *face of the pages* is made in type-metal.

" This stereotyping, or making *solid* pages of type from pages composed of *movable* type, is a most simple but useful and ingenious process. It is only needful to make a hollow, or mould, from the type, and then to pour into that mould melted type-metal, and the thing is done.

D

"This mould used to be formed by pouring plaster of Paris on to the type; but it is now chiefly made of *papier mache.* Several sheets of thin paper, that have for some days been well moistened, are glued slightly together by a particular paste made for the purpose. The surface of the paper is covered lightly over with French chalk, to prevent any clinging to the type, and then laid over the pages of type. A stout piece of paper, or a piece of cotton cloth, is put over the layers of paper, and the paper beaten with a hard brush. When thoroughly beaten in, the paper and type are put under a press, and afterwards placed on a hot iron table to be dried. As soon as dry, the mould is taken off the type and placed in the 'casting-box.' This casting-box is made of two parts, joined by a hinge. The mould is placed in one half, and the other half fastened down over it; there is just space left between the two for the required thickness of the plate. The melted type-metal is poured in at one end, and sets directly. These stereotype plates are not thicker than one-sixth of an inch, and are fastened on to metal or wooden blocks, so that the plate and the block together are the exact height of the real type."

"But what is the particular good of this stereotyping?" asked the Elzevir. "What use do these plates of solid type answer? Can you *print* from them?"

"O yes; quite as well as from the real type. These fictitious types not only save a great deal of the wear and tear of the 'founts,' but they also prevent the necessity of keeping the type standing for copies of a work that may afterwards be wanted. Then, also, any number of plates can be cast from the same type, and these plates can be sent away and printed at different places at the same time. You can see, therefore, how easily copies of a work may, by the aid of this process, be multiplied and circulated."

"It is a great pity that the old clergyman of whom our late owner used to speak did not know of this invention; it would have saved him a great deal of time," said the Great Folio. "This gentleman, in the course of fourteen years (from 1795 to 1809), wrote and printed with his own hands twenty-six volumes of 'A System of Divinity.'"

"But why did he not get it printed for him; there were surely plenty of printers willing to do it?" said the New Book.

"Ah, but he was *poor*, and could not afford the expense of having it printed.

So he bought old type, and he and his housekeeper set it up between them. He could only manage to set up two pages at a time, print those two, and then 'distribute' the type, and use it for the next two pages, and so on."

" But what a labour ! Did he really get it all printed in that slow way ?" said the New Book.

" Yes ; night and day he worked with a zeal that nothing could daunt, a patience that nothing could exhaust, in his quiet parsonage in Devonshire, under the shadow of the Dartmoor hills. Fourteen copies of his work were printed, and one of them has a resting-place, I have heard, in the Bodleian Library."

" Well, it deserves to be kept in so honourable a place, as a memorial of what patient labour can effect," said the Quarto. " I should much like to see the book, and learn what the merits of ' The System of Divinity' really are."

"They must, at any rate, have been considerable in the writer's own eyes," said the Esop. " Pray, when was this most ingenious method of creating pages of type found out ? "

"A Mr. William Ged, a goldsmith at Edinburgh, first suggested the idea, about 1725. But the printers and compositors of his day, most absurdly, set themselves against the invention, and poor Ged was very unfairly treated among them. He failed, died, and left the secret to his son, who also failed ; and the idea seems to have been forgotten or neglected for half a century, till Lord Stanhope, to whom the art of printing is under great obligations, revived it. In 1816, Professor Cowper took out a patent for *curving* stereotype plates, which was a great step in a direction full of importance, as you will see more fully as we advance in the history of the art. In 1853, Dr. Wilson, at a meeting of the Royal Society of Arts, called attention to the process of making *papier-maché* moulds for the stereotype plates ; and, in 1856, Mr. Walter of the *Times* and an Italian named Dellagana made great improvements in the process, and in the method of *curving* the matrix, or mould. The *papier-maché* mould has many advantages over the old plaster of Paris mould. The materials required are simple ; the whole process only takes one hour, while the old process took six hours ; the mould is not so easily broken, and can be used again, while the one made of plaster of Paris could only be used once."

D 2

CHAPTER III.

ENGRAVING.

"AND now, if you have no objection, I should like to say a little about my engravings, which form no inconsiderable part of my attractions, if I may be pardoned the expression," resumed the New Book, after a pause.

"Yes; pictures, if they are good, add very greatly to the value of a book, whether it be a printed or a manuscript one," said the French MS., who possessed a number of beautiful miniatures done in grisaille, and was really a good specimen of early French art.

"But your ladyship's pictures are painted by hand on the vellum itself," remarked the New Book; "while engravings, as you know, doubtless, are *impressions* taken from either *raised* lines, as in wood engravings, or from *sunken* lines, as in copper and steel."

"Working in metal was an art known in very early days," said the Elzévir. "There were many skilled workers in metal among the Jews, and they most probably learned the art from their Egyptian masters."

"But, still, as was remarked by the learned and venerable Folio, it never seems to have struck the ancients that they might put ink, or some similar substance, on to their carvings, and thus take impressions from the metal on to another substance."

"And it was not till the fifteenth century that the art of engraving, strictly speaking, became known and practised in *Europe*," remarked the Elzevir. "It is said that a native of Florence, a goldsmith, named Finiguerra, discovered it, about 1460. He was accustomed, like the jewellers of his day, to engrave figures

ENGRAVING ON COPPER AND STEEL.

upon church ornaments; then to fill in the cut lines with a black substance, a mixture of silver and lead dissolved in borax and sulphur; and to take impressions from the metal in clay and sulphur. The black mixture was called *Niello*, and the term became applied to the art itself. As this Finiguerra was à clever man, the idea struck him that impressions might be taken upon *paper* as well as on the sulphur mould."

"Excuse my interrupting you," said the Esop. "I know it is the custom to give Florence the pre-eminence in the discovery of the art of copper engraving; but, I believe, it can be proved that the art was known and practised in Upper Germany before it was in Italy. Our great Martin Schöngauer died in 1486, and left behind him an immense number of engravings; and it stands to reason that some of them must have been executed before this Maso Finiguerra made his discovery."

"But there were charts engraved and printed at *Rome* in the year 1478; were there not?" asked the Quarto.

"Yes; but they were done by two *Germans*," replied the Esop—"Conrad Sweynheim and another man, whose name I forget."

"The truth of the matter most likely is," said the Great Folio, "that the discovery was made in both countries much about the same time. The introduction of the 'rolling-press,' as it used to be termed, whether by this Finiguerra or others, greatly facilitated the taking of impressions from the engraved copper plate. I know that many people say that we in England knew nothing about the use of this 'roller-press' till one Mr. John Speed, in the reign of King James the First, brought over the knowledge from Antwerp. But I think they must be mistaken, for I have heard our late owner declare that he had seen maps that were printed between the years 1574 and 1579; maps that had been executed by one Christopher Saxton, to whom Queen Elizabeth gave a patent, in the nineteenth year of her reign, to survey and *engrave on copper* all the counties of England. In her reign, however, a celebrated man, a native of Antwerp, settled in England, and advanced the knowledge of the rolling-press among us. The art of penmanship owes a great deal to this invention, for copy-books and specimens of fine curious writing were after that time printed by the rolling-press."

"And the great Albrecht Dürer," said the Quarto; "he engraved a great deal upon copper; did he not?"

"Yes; indeed, our great master engraved more on copper than even on wood, celebrated as he is in that last branch of art. Painter, sculptor, poet, man

PRINTING FROM STEEL AND COPPER PLATES AT THE "ROLLER" PRESS.

of letters, engraver —in what did he not excel?" exclaimed the Esop, in a burst of enthusiasm.

"Perhaps you will favour us with a few particulars about him and his chief works?" said the New Book.

Nothing loth, the Esop began : "Albrecht Dürer was born at Nuremberg, in 1471. His father was a goldsmith, and a clever, though not by any means a rich, man. He taught young Albrecht the elements of drawing, for he could use cleverly both chalk and pencil, and wished his son to follow his own craft. But the lad petitioned to be brought up as an artist, not as a goldsmith."

"Goldsmiths seem always to be clever, and generally wealthy," remarked the Law Book ; "witness Fust at Mentz, and Finiguerra at Florence."

"Clever? Yes. It is a singular fact that all the earliest engravers, both in Italy and Germany, were goldsmiths or the sons of goldsmiths. The training and practice of their particular craft, by the exactness of eye and the carefulness of hand which it required, must have been a good preparation for their further progress in higher art. And, as a general rule, the goldsmiths were held in high *social* esteem. In a procession that took place at Antwerp in the year 1520, the order was in this wise—goldsmiths, painters, builders, silk embroiderers, sculptors, joiners, carpenters, sailors, fishermen, masons, tanners, clothworkers, bakers, tailors, shoemakers, shopkeepers, and merchants ; then the shooters, cavaliers, and city guards. It is a curious specimen of gradation of rank, and shows that Antwerp had some very peculiar notions of her own on that point ; for, though other cities would give a forward place to the goldsmiths, few, if any, would have placed the cavaliers where she did."

"Where were the *authors?*" said the New Book.

"Ah, that particular description of being either did not exist in numbers sufficient to form a class, or it was not considered sufficiently *respectable* for a civic procession. But to go back to the young Dürer. His father yielded to his wishes, and placed him with the painter Wohlgemuth for three years. Afterwards he became the pupil of Martin Schöngauer—called Martin Schön, or Hubsche Martin, Martin the Beautiful, or Martin the Skilful—painter and engraver, living at Colmar, a place forty-two miles south of my own town, Strasburg : a worthy master for a fitting pupil. At twenty-three Albrecht married, and settled with his young wife Agnes in a new house in the Zisselgrasse, opposite the Thiergärten Gate—a large commodious house, with a door wide enough for a pack-horse to go in. On the right of the hall was a very small room, where the young master thought and worked ; though, of course, he had a large one for the workpeople and pupils under his immediate eye. The upper front room was a grand room, looking out upon the 'Place' and the high tower that protected the castle-gate. I wonder whether the house still stands ?"

ALBRECHT DÜRER.

"It was so standing, I have heard, in 1828 ; for a bronze statue by Rauch was then erected at the foot of the Zisselgasse, and the name of the street changed to Dürerstrasse," said the New Book. "Nuremberg honours the memory of her illustrious son."

"Nuremberg does well so to do," replied the Esop. "In that house were done, at least designed, most of the master's greatest works. And labour he did—the number of his works is overwhelming—one wonders when he found

time to eat and to sleep.   To take but one period of his life as an instance—from
1507 to 1514—the number of his works executed was above a hundred, and
among them some of his finest, such as 'The Little Passion,' a set of sixteen
miniature designs on copper, remarkable for their elaborateness, their delicately
minute details; and 'The Knight with Death and the Devil,' the most wonderful artistic conception Germany can show, and which puzzled men in my day
to explain, and, I dare say, puzzles men in this day."

   "What is there in it so very mysterious and inexplicable?" asked the
New Book.

   "Nothing, but a fully-armed old soldier, carrying a long lance on a strong
war-horse: both man and horse have evidently seen hard service.   Death rides on
a little horse by the side of the knight, and a *dog* follows behind them.   Now,
you know, the dog in northern nations does not bear the best of characters.   He
is a lineal descendant of *Fenrir*, the wolf who swallowed Odin himself; and he
is generally looked upon as having an intimate connection with the powers of
evil—evil bodily, and evil spiritual.   So it does not speak well for the knight that
this dog is so close upon his heels.   Some people think the picture represents the
true knight—one that will fight against all evil, and overcome at last; others,
that it represents the *robber* knight—one that was a disgrace to all the virtues
that we consider ought to belong to the knight—the avenger—the deliverer.
Germany used, in former days, to be much troubled with this latter kind of false
knight—one who cared for nothing save plunder and bloodshed.   However, the
great master left no key to the riddle, so it must remain unread.   But I was
going to remark that the patience and the care bestowed upon his smallest studies,
as well as upon his greatest pictures, are as remarkable as his industry and the
rapidity of his execution.   Nothing was *too* small for careful study—the head of
a stag, a table, a fireplace, no matter what; if he required it as a part of his
picture, or was struck by its own individual beauty—as the wing of a bird, for
instance, of which he made several studies—it became the object of his loving,
careful study.

   "Nuremberg has much to interest all lovers of the antique and picturesque
united; with its old wall and seventy round and square towers; with its eight

gates and its ancient castle; and justly proud are the Nurembergers of their city, declaring that—

> ' Nürnberg's hand geht durch alle land.'
> ' Nuremberg's hand goes through every land.'

But though it may not be as much thought of now as it used to be in earlier times, yet, I imagine, that always, and through all ages, it must be world-renowned as being the birthplace of the great artist Albrecht Dürer."

"Indeed, I think with you," replied the New Book. "All artists, and all persons with artistic feelings, venerate the name of Albrecht Dürer. May I tell you how a modern poet sings of him, and of his native city, Nuremberg?—

> ' Here, when art was still religion, with a simple, reverent heart,
> Lived and laboured Albrecht Dürer, the Evangelist of Art:
> Hence, in silence and in sorrow, toiling still with busy hand,
> Like an emigrant, he wandered, seeking for the Better Land.
> *Emigravit,* is the inscription on the tomb-stone where he lies;
> Dead he is not,—but departed,—for the Artist never dies.
> Fairer seems the ancient city, and the sunshine seems more fair,
> That he once has trod its pavement, that he once has breathed its air!
> Not thy Councils, not thy Kaisers, win for thee the world's regard;
> But thy painter, Albrecht Dürer, and Hans Sachs, thy cobbler-bard.'" *

Quite a cloud of dust was raised by the clapping which testified the approval by the book society of these sentiments of the American poet. When it had subsided, the Esop resumed :—

"The name of Hans Sachs, that poet-shoemaker, brings back to mind so many other illustrious names of men with whom our Albrecht must have been familiar; clever, skilful citizens of Nuremberg. There was Peter Vischer, the smith; Adam Kraft, the sculptor; Sebastian Lindermast, the red-smith—*i.e.*, the worker in copper; Veit Stoss, the carver in wood. Nuremberg was famous, also, at that time, for its clever inventors in mechanical matters. There was Peter Henleim, who invented the pocket clock, the ' Nürnberger Eier'—the Nuremberg

---

* Longfellow.

Egg—as it was called; and Bullmann, the locksmith and clockmaker. The Emperor Charles V. had such a high opinion of this Bullmann, that he had him brought all the way in a sedan chair to Vienna, to put his Majesty's watch to rights.

"Then Nuremberg had its *literary* society, if you please. There was Albrecht's godfather, Koberger, who, in 1493, printed and published the *Chronicon* (the *Nuremberg Chronicle*), which was illustrated by Wohlgemuth, Conrad Celtes, and Pirkheimer, the friend of Albrecht, and his two learned sisters; Johann Cochlaüs, the opponent of the Reformation; and Jerome Baumgärten, friend and scholar of the saintly Melancthon; and numbers of others whose names I could mention. That Conrad Celtes formed the first German literary association, which was called the 'Sodalitas Literaria Rhenana.' I have no doubt you moderns have many similar associations; but, you see, you are not the only clever and literary people. And we must not forget the seven 'Little Masters,' as they were termed—the clever artist men who gathered round our Dürer, either as pupils or as companions; some of them natives of Nuremberg, some of neighbouring towns, who settled there, attracted by the fame of the great master, and who spread abroad his name and influence in after days and other lands."

"And other towns besides Nuremberg can boast of their clever men," said the Elzevir; "Amsterdam, Antwerp, Leyden, and many others, can show a long roll of illustrious names."

"No doubt of it, my good friend; no doubt of it," said the Great Folio. "And if needs were, England could contribute her subsidy to the illustrious host; but we shall exhaust the patience of our young friend, who is kindly prepared to show us the modern methods of executing the various kinds of engraving."

"Will you tell us first how engraving on copper is done?" said the English MS.

"The plate of copper must be coated over with wax," resumed the New Book. "An outline drawing of that which is to be engraved must be first made upon thin transparent paper ('tracing paper'), the paper turned face downwards upon the plate, and the lines of the drawing transferred by pressure to the plate. The engraver, with a fine steel point, goes over the lines lightly, so as to pierce the wax and scratch the copper. The wax is then melted off, and the engraver may begin his work. For it he will require three principal tools—a 'graver,' or *burin*, made of steel, by which he cuts the lines into the copper; a 'burnisher,' a smooth tool, three inches long, by which he softens down the lines; and a 'scraper,' six inches long, to remove the little ridges or 'burrs' of copper, which his graver makes as it ploughs its way over the metal. The description takes a short time enough, but the work itself is slow and tedious, and requires the engraver to be a man of much skill and knowledge."

"Then how is the *printing* from the copper managed?" asked the English MS.

"That is a very simple matter," replied the New Book. "The copper plate is well daubed over with ink till all the lines are well filled. Of course, a great deal of ink goes where it is not wanted. This has to be most carefully cleaned off; and the constant rubbing of the plate, to take off the superfluous ink after each daubing, wears the plate very much. The properly inked and cleaned plate is covered with a damp sheet of paper, passed under a roller, on which is a blanket-cloth, and the impression is made upon the paper."

"Then what are *steel* engravings; are they very different?" inquired the French MS.

"Not as to the way in which the engravings are executed upon them," replied the New Book. "Steel plates are more serviceable than copper, because they can yield more impressions without wearing out. You may take 50,000 impressions from a steel plate, and yet the plate be very little the worse. Steel engraving is said to be indebted for its establishment to a Mr. Jacob Perkins, who invented a way of making steel soft by de-carbonising it, and then, when the engraving had been made, re-hardening it again; but, I believe, it is not now considered necessary to do this—at least for picture engraving."

"I always thought that engravings on copper and steel were done somehow by means of acid, some very strong acid," said the French MS.

"You are thinking of aquafortis, that is, nitric acid, which is used in the kind of engraving called *etching*. In etching, the copper or plate is first of all coated over with a mixture of bees-wax and Burgundy pitch. Now, wherever that coating is placed the acid cannot take effect. The drawing made with a black-lead pencil upon transparent paper is transferred to the plate, and the engraver, taking an 'etching-needle,' a needle resembling a common one, placed in a handle four or five inches long, carefully goes over the lines, removing the wax and scratching the copper. A border of wax, half an inch high, is laid all round the plate, so as to form a sort of trough, and into this trough the aquafortis, that is, nitric acid, is poured. Wherever the etching-needle has removed the wax the acid *bites* in and dissolves the copper.

"Now," continued the New Book, "it would never do to have all the lines in a picture of the same strength, and to have no gradations of light and shade. The different tints are produced in this way. The parts that are to remain faint are 'stopped out,' as it is termed, after the first wash of the acid. They have a coating of lamp-black and Venice-turpentine applied to them by a camel-hair brush; and this mixture, known as the 'stopping-ground,' effectually stops any more acid that may be put on from touching those parts. These processes of 'stopping out' and of pouring on the acid are repeated as many times as there are gradations of light and shade in the picture. You can judge how much the engraver needs to possess artistic feeling and knowledge, in order to produce a good picture from his copper plate."

"Ah, the invention of this etching process is due to Lucas of Leyden," said the Elzevir.

"Perhaps so, if it can be called an *invention*," retorted the Esop. "It was the custom of armourers and other workers in metal to use corrosive acids, so it was easy enough to apply the idea to engraving for prints. Albrecht Dürer etched about nine plates, though I confess they are not the best of his works. He does not seem to have kept the acid longer on one part than another—to have learnt the way and use of 'stopping out,' as our friend called it. Dürer etched on iron and pewter plates as well as copper. Nothing came amiss to his hand. He made great use of the 'dry point,' as it was termed—that is, using the end of the etching-needle for scratching and scribbling, and leaving the raised 'burr' upon the plate, which, when it was printed, gave a smudgy effect, that answered well for light tints. Rembrandt, I have heard, used to do the same, with admirable results."

"We use the same term 'dry point' for the same process in the present day, and with the same good results," said the New Book, "as was the case with the artists in past days. Many of our modern artists understand how to *engrave* as well as paint; and superintend, if they do not execute, the engravings of their pictures. A friend of mine saw, the other day, three proof engravings of a picture of our celebrated Turner's, and on the margin of the prints were some remarks and suggestions to the engraver in Turner's own hand. It is well known that Turner engraved some of his pictures himself. In 'stippling,' a process of which some of you may have heard, the drawing is executed by *dots* instead of lines, and the acid eats into the dots. Some people like the effect produced; I do not think much of it myself. Stippling, mezzotinto, aquatinta, are really only modifications in the process of etching; the principle being much the same in all."

"Mezzotinto! Has not Prince Rupert, the nephew of King Charles I., the credit of discovering that particular method of engraving, reckless soldier that he was?" inquired the Virgil.

"Yes," replied the Great Folio; "it is said that he was watching a soldier clean a very rusty gun, when he noticed that the impression left on the paper was the strongest just in the places where the rust had been scraped away the most. Being a bit of a philosopher, he thought of applying the fact to engraving. It seemed to him that if the plate to be engraved upon were first *roughed over* as the gun was with rust, and then the lights scraped away more or less, a good effect might be produced. The prince tried to do this with a roller that had small grooves in it, and succeeded to some extent."

"That was an ingenious application of a chance observation, and showed that the prince's mind must have occupied itself with that and kindred subjects. But it must not be forgotten that an engraver living at the same time thought of the same kind of thing, though he produced the roughened surface with a *file*, instead of a grooved roller," remarked the Law Book. "But how is this mezzotinto done at the present day?"

"The main idea is the same," replied the New Book. "The plate is covered all over with minute scratches by means of a toothed tool, so that the whole would, if printed, give a dark ground. Then the parts intended to be light in the picture are scraped away.

"Many of my companions," continued the New Book, after a short pause, "possessed illustrations of great beauty that had been *drawn on stone*—lithographed. Now, lithography is a department of the arts that will not, I fancy, be familiar to any of the present company; its discovery is of too recent a date."

"I notice that you say *drawn*, not *engraved*, upon the stone. Have you a reason for laying stress on the word *drawn?*" inquired the Law Book, who, true to his profession, was on the watch for verbal errors.

"You are right; I had a reason for using the word *drawn* with an emphasis," replied the New Book. "Because in lithographs the impression has been produced upon the paper by lines that have simply been *drawn upon* the stone—not *sunk in* by acid, or *cut in* by the graver, as in steel and copper engravings; nor have they been *raised in relief*, as in the process of *wood engraving*. Do you see the difference?"

"Yes; and I am curious to hear how the work is done," replied the Law Book, "and when and by whom the discovery was made."

"The art of taking impressions from drawings made on stone was discovered by a musician of Munich, one Aloys Senefelder, quite at the close of the eighteenth century. It is said that he discovered it by an accident; but so-called accidents are only of use to people who know how to employ their eyes, and are accustomed to think about what they see," replied the New Book.

"A very true and sensible observation, my young friend," said the Great Folio; "but will you kindly tell us what the accidental occurrence was which led the musician to this discovery?"

"It is said that this Aloys Senefelder was very poor—so poor that he could not pay for the engraving of his own musical compositions; so, perhaps, his poverty helped to quicken his faculties. At any rate, he tried a little engraving on his own account. One day his mother asked him to put down some account, and having no paper at hand, he wrote the memorandum upon a piece of *stone* lying near, with his compositor's ink; and then the idea struck him that he might raise the letters by corroding away the surrounding stone, and then print from it with a small press which he possessed. One thing led on to another, till, by degrees, he discovered the method of taking impressions from the simple drawing on the stone; but, most likely, without understanding the principles on which it is based."

"Pray, what may these principles be?" said the Mystery. "You moderns are always trying to find out the *principles* on which a matter depends. You are never easy till you find out a reason for things, in the things themselves."

"The duty of science is to find out, *where possible*, the mysterious—that is to say, the unknown," replied the New Book.

"The principles on which the art of lithography is based are—that resinous and greasy compounds readily *adhere* to a particular kind of limestone; that this limestone and its greasy compounds, when *united*, will very readily receive *ink*, while they refuse to have anything to do with water. But the limestone, when it has no greasy substances adhering to it, will absorb water with ease. Now, the drawings that are put upon these particular limestones are done either with an ink or a kind of chalk that is of a soapy or greasy nature. The materials are much the same in both—lard, white soap, white wax, lamp-black, and shellac. A little potash or carbonate of soda is added in the case of the chalk. Now, this greasy compound adheres firmly to the stone. When the drawing has been made on the stone, the stone is washed with a weak solution of sulphuric acid, which acid dissolves out the alkali, having, as our friend the Mystery will know, a great affinity for potash and soda; and the undissolved compound is left on the stone. The whole stone is then washed with water. The parts where there is no chalk or ink *absorb* the water; the parts where the chalk lies resist the water. The printing-ink is then applied, which clings to the chalky part, but *not to the other*; paper is placed over the stone, and impressions taken by the press in much the ordinary way. The coloured lithographs, called chromo-lithographs, are done in the same sort of way—only that for each different colour there will have to be a separate stone. The best stones, suitable for the purpose of drawing upon, are procured from the quarries near Pappenheim, on the Danube, in Bavaria; but useful stones are also to be found in England, France, Canada, and one or two other places."

E

" Are illustrations produced in the way you have just described considered to be better than steel or wood engravings?" asked the Esop.

" Perhaps not for general purposes," replied the New Book; " but, in my own opinion, a lithograph has some special advantages over other forms of illustrations.

" In drawing on stone, the means employed are so simple and so closely resembling those used by the artist on paper or canvas, that the lithographer is able to reproduce the various effects of light and shade, and the special characteristics of the original picture, with greater truthfulness than can be done by the engraver on steel or wood, who has to make use of an entirely different set of ways and means to attain his object.

" I need not stop to point out the evident and great service rendered to the world by the art of engraving. A painting is but *one* of a kind, and can be enjoyed only by the comparative few, even when it is placed in a public gallery. But reproductions, by the means of engravings, of the works of ancient and modern artists, place the picture, in a certain degree, within the reach of the multitude, and spread abroad the love and knowledge of true art. An engraving is to the picture what the concave lens is to the focus—it *diffuses* the light which would otherwise remain concentrated in a point.

" My own engravings were executed on *wood*, as you will easily perceive by examining them."

" I also am adorned with wood-cuts," said the Senior Defoe, displaying, with some ostentation, his queer faded drawings.

" And so am I also,". said the Spenser; " and my engravings are thought to possess a good deal of merit. My author, Edmund Spenser, would, I think, have been pleased with them."

" Very likely he might," replied the New Book; " for illustrations to books were not so common in the days of Spenser as they were when Mr. John Ball published you. I see, also, that your twelve pictures all bear the name of Fourdrinier as their artist. Now, as you were printed in the year 1732, it appears to me that your Fourdrinier must have been an ancestor of the celebrated firm of Messrs. Fourdrinier, who were the first to take up and carry out the idea of making an endless web of paper by machinery, which idea came originally from France.

But, if you and my respected relative will pardon my saying so, the ideas of the present day as to perspective, and light and shade, and the drawing of figures, are certainly somewhat different from those which were entertained when your illustrations were made.

"Our artists think it desirable to make a distinction in size between the men and the trees in their pictures; and they do not run the roads up into the sky, as I see they have in many of your drawings. It is evident your illustrations were done before the days of Thomas Bewick, who lived in the latter part of the eighteenth century. He greatly improved the art of wood engraving; and ever since his efforts it has progressed rapidly, and has now reached a high degree of excellence.

"You see," continued the New Book, "it is essential, absolutely essential, that an engraver, whatever be the material on which he engraves, should be *an artist.* Whether he employs other hands or not, he ought himself to be able to design, and to draw his design upon his block or plate; and the more correctly he is able to outline, and the more thoroughly he understands the true principles of light and shade, so much the better will he be able to produce a *good engraving.* Of course, there are definite and special ways of bringing about the desired results. Engraving, like every other art, has its own particular limitations and conditions, which must be thoroughly understood and mastered before even the best artist can create the effects he desires.

"In painting and drawing the means are almost unlimited; such diversity of effects can be produced by lines and differences of *colour*, and any mistakes can be easily set right; but in engraving it is far otherwise. The engraver can produce his effects only by *variations in the markings of the lines;* on their lightness or their strength, and on the way they are arranged."

"It must be much more pleasant to be an artist and sit down, as mine used to do, and draw and paint away just as he liked, without thinking of anything except his own wishes. Genius ought never to be cramped and bound by rules and conditions," remarked the French MS.

"Ah, but your ladyship must remember," rejoined the New Book, "that *true genius can never be bound.* Rules and restrictions, that are fetters and hindrances to mere skill and talent, are but as the guiding reins to real genius.

F 2

The true Pegasus shows his divine descent, and proves himself worthy of his wings, by the grace and ease with which he *folds them*. But now to come to wood engraving of the present day.

"In an engraving on wood the lines and figures are left *raised*, the surrounding parts being cut away," continued the New Book; "while in engraving on steel and copper the lines are *sunk in*. You see, an engraving on wood is really, to all intents and purposes, *a type*; and the great advantage of this kind of engravings is, that the blocks can be 'imposed' and printed together with the letter-press, and impressions consequently taken with great rapidity. For that among other reasons, wood-cuts are more common than other kinds of engravings."

"Will wood of any kind do for the purpose of engraving?" asked the English MS.

"No. The wood used for engraving is procured from the box-tree, because the grain of that wood is exceedingly fine. The 'blocks,' as the pieces of wood are called, are always made one inch in thickness; and you will see the reason for that when I tell you they are printed with *the type*, and consequently must stand on a level with it. The box-tree will not furnish blocks that are more than six or eight inches square; so, if a large picture is wanted, we are obliged to join two or more pieces together. A pound of wood makes a printing block about six inches square. A wood engraver does not need a complicated set of tools. He must have a pad of leather, stuffed with sand, on which to rest the block. Then he must have 'gravers,' of six or eight degrees of fineness,—a graver is a tool made of steel, with a small head or handle of wood—the steel part is about four inches long; 'tint-tools,' in order to cut parallel lines close together, to represent sky-tints,—tint-tools differ in fineness, and are thinner in the blade, and more tapering at the point than the gravers; a 'flat' or 'gouge tool,' to cut away blank spaces; a 'hone,' on which to sharpen his instruments; and a steel 'burnisher.'

"The first thing to be done (that is, after rubbing a little moistened whiting and bath-brick over the block, to produce a good surface upon it) is to make a drawing upon the block of that which has to be engraved. If the artist can draw it *at once* upon the block—the *reverse* way, of course, to that which it will appear in the engraving—all the better; for no *traced* drawing has quite the same ease and spirit in its lines that a free-hand drawing has. But if not, then a tracing must be made on thin paper; the paper turned face downwards on the block, and the lines marked over with some pointed tool, with just sufficient pressure to leave the mark upon the surface of the block. In engraving a wood-cut, you must remember that wherever the pencil has made a mark, or produced a *tint, that part must be left ;* and the parts that are not touched by the pencil or brush must be cut away. The parts *left* will print more or less black ; the parts *cut away* will be white in the finished picture. Sometimes the shading in a drawing that is to be copied for an engraving is done, not by lines in pencil, but by *tints* or washes in Indian ink. Now the engraver has to consider in what kind of way he can best produce the effect of the different tints, the light and shade of the picture."

"But how will he manage ? he can but cut away the wood or leave the wood, that I see," said the French MS. "How can he make different degrees of darkness?"

"If the engraver leaves a piece of the wood standing up altogether untouched by his graver, then, of course, that piece, large or small, will be *quite* black in the printed cut. Of course, that will do for some parts—the deep shades ; but it would never do for the tints of the sky, for instance. The different degrees of darkness are produced by the difference in the thickness of the lines that *are left*, and by the width of the spaces *cut away* between the lines. The great aim of an engraver on wood should be to have a bold, clear outline, and to produce the light and shade by as few and simple lines as possible. It is easy in his own studio to take proofs, with fine printing-ink and India paper, that shall represent very delicate lines ; but when those same blocks come to be printed on the ordinary book paper, and by a cylinder and inking apparatus, that goes on with the work regardless whether they are printing type or pictures, all the delicate lines will appear blurred and messed, to the great annoyance of the artist; where fewer, clearer, and bolder lines would have come out well and sharply."

"Wood engraving must have greatly altered from what it was in my day," said the Æsop. "The engraver on wood in my country was called the 'formschneider ;' perhaps because he cut the wood and prepared it to be printed with the type in the ' formes ;' or perhaps because of the small pictures, the figures of saints and others, which in those early days of *printed* pictures were thought very much of. Then there was none of the fine work that your pictures show, and none of that skill and judgment required that you speak of as essential to a wood engraver, and to all engravers. The formschneider had only to *cut away* all the wood on which there were no lines, and only, or chiefly, used a fine knife as his tool."

" But surely Albrecht Dürer improved the art ; did he not ?" inquired the New Book.

" Most surely he did," replied the Esop. " He re-made the art, or rather, from a rough mechanical employment he raised it to an art. Not that he actually *engraved much*, if at all, upon the wood ; but then he *drew upon the wood*, and his correct and spirited drawing compelled the formschneider, whether he would or not, into the production of better results than formerly. Another thing struck me while our young friend was speaking, and that was the difference in the wood used. In my day the wood engraver used pear-tree and other woods, and the blocks were cut and used in the *plank ;* while it seems the moderns only use the wood of the box-tree, and cut it sectionally, so that they can only get small blocks, the box-tree being of small growth. That would not have suited our Dürer at all, for in his ' Triumphal Arch ' for the Emperor Maximilian he used ninety-two blocks, in some of which you may see the seams of the plank running from end to end ; and these ninety-two blocks formed together an engraved surface of eleven feet three inches by ten wide. What would your modern wood engravers think of that ?"

" Well, I can hardly think such very large blocks could be best suited for engraving," replied the New Book.

" Perhaps not. I dare say the largeness was to please his imperial patron. Certainly, the Emperor took great interest in the progress of this gigantic work, for he used to visit the artist and the head formschneider, Jerome Rosch, almost daily. But Dürer did many other works ; for instance, a set of twelve blocks, size fifteen inches by ten and three-quarters, representing incidents in the Lord's life, and called ' The Greater Passion ;' and a set of thirty-seven blocks, size five inches by three and seven-eighths, called ' The Lesser Passion.' "

" He must have had a great many men under his direction, employed in executing his numerous works on wood," remarked the Elzevir.

" Yes, indeed. The formschneiders of Nuremberg, during Albrecht Dürer's life, were a very numerous body. And there was at least *one* woman among them, for there is a portrait by the master of a blue-eyed, round-faced girl of the *bourgeoisie*, and on the picture is the name ' Fronica—Formschneiderin.' She surely ought to be made the patron saint of all lady wood engravers, if any such there are, not so much for her own particular virtues, as from the fact that she must have had some training from the master himself."

" Wood engraving is a department of art well suited to ladies, and is practised by many with good success. It is, or was, taught in some at least of our schools of art; and it seems a pity that it should not be more followed by the lady students as a profession. But the fact is, that when they have gone through the necessary artistic training, without which no one ought to think of being an engraver, students are apt to turn to the large canvas and the brush, as being the more fascinating and the more remunerative," replied the New Book.

" Those block-books, the ' Biblia Pauperum,' that have been mentioned, must be curious. I have never seen one; I suppose they are not often to be met with ?" said the French MS.

" They are, indeed, both rare and curious," replied the Elzevir. " They were printed on one side of the paper only, and the blank sides of the pages were glued together, so that they appeared as a book. One of these block-books is known to have consisted of forty leaves, small folio ; printed, of course, from the same number of blocks. I have heard that £50 have been given for some of the worst copies of these books, and as much as £250 for a good one."

" The little pictures, the figures of saints, some of the earliest attempts in Europe at picture painting, were very highly esteemed and widely circulated. They called them ' helgen ' in my country, and in France they went, I believe, by the name of ' dominos,' " said the Esop.

" And funny little things were many of those said ' dominos,' " said the French MS.; " and in order to preserve their existence, they were often pasted into written books."

"They could hardly be stranger than some of the drawings in the MSS. themselves, I should think," said the Æsop. "But I must confess the illuminations we find in some MSS. are exceedingly beautiful; and your ladyship's miniatures are invaluable."

"I once heard our late owner," said the Great Folio, "talk about a present that had been made to the place you call the 'Bodleian Library' of sixty-one elephant folio volumes, comprising Clarendon's 'History of the Rebellion,' of his 'Life,' and of Bishop Burnet's 'History of his own Times;' and he said that these volumes were illustrated and *interleaved* with no less than 19,244 drawings and engravings of every person in any way connected with the matter in the books. There are actually 743 portraits of Charles I., 373 of Cromwell, 552 of Charles II., 309 views of London, and 166 of Westminster."

"Whoever made the collection would take a long time over it, I should think," said the English MS.

"Yes; I understood that it was begun in 1795, and the volumes were presented in 1839," replied the Great Folio.

"And not so very long ago a book was sold that had belonged to an old gentleman at Kensington, which was interleaved in a similar way," said the New Book. "It was, so I heard, a copy of 'Childe Harold,' and had been printed expressly for this gentleman, and in it he had placed all kinds of engravings."

"I believe that one of the very earliest, if not the earliest, of wood-cuts, to which a positive date (1423) is affixed, was found in the cover of a Latin MS. of the date of 1417. This MS. belonged to the most ancient convent of Germany, the Chartreuse of Buxheim, Memminguon. It is a picture of St. Christopher carrying the child Christ, and a most curious thing it is. I am afraid our young friend with his beautiful engravings would greatly despise it," said the Folio.

"Perhaps I might be tempted to smile, and to think that the wood-cut did not do justice to the beautiful legend," replied the New Book.

"The cut was as good as the legend," said some Book from the background.

"Well, I confess," said the New Book, "that I was much pleased with the legend. I heard it from one of my friends, who received it direct from a lady who liked to gather up and condense the floating legends of the early saints."

"Would you oblige us with the modern version of that story?" said the Great Folio.

"Willingly," replied the New Book, "though, of course, I cannot repeat it verbatim; I can only transfer to you the impression left on my mind.

"St. Christopher, whose name at first was, as you know, Offero, *the bearer*, was a heathen, but a strong-hearted, brave, genuine man, with more physical strength and muscle than he well knew what to do with. Being so strong himself, he resolved that he would serve none but the strongest master— one that could conquer, but never be conquered. So he searched and inquired everywhere, received many directions, and made many mistakes. At last, from some things he heard related of the Christ the Christians worshipped, he concluded that he was the Master of whom he was in search. Christ's servant he would be. Offero inquired what he must do in order to prove his fealty; how he must *serve* Christ. The holy man to whom he applied told him that he must *pray* and meditate. But this was not at all the kind of thing to suit Offero, strong man that he was. So he said to the holy man, 'I cannot pray to your Christ, but I can work for him.' Now the holy man being, fortunately, also a *wise* man, immediately appointed Offero to some downright hard bodily work— which was to help people across a most dangerous ford, that had to be crossed in order to reach one of the churches, as well as for other purposes. It was work requiring courage, energy, patience, and constant attention. It just suited our heathen. One night, when the wind was at its highest, and the waters raged their fiercest, a child's voice was heard crying for help. Offero gave it. At peril of his life he bore the child across the whirl of water. More than once his strong man's strength had failed him, great as it was, had not his still stronger devotion to his duty sustained him. Safe on land, the child whom he had carried revealed himself as Christ his Lord. 'Thou art my faithful servant,' said the Christ; 'thou hast not known how to *pray* to me, but right well hast thou found out the way to *work* for me. Henceforth thy name shall be known as CHRISTOPHER, the CHRIST BEARER.' And the strong man bowed his head and bent his knee. From that time forth he knew not only how to *work*, but also how to *worship*."

CHAPTER IV.

ELECTROTYPING—PHOTOGRAPHY.

"Before I quite leave the subject of engraving," said the New Book, "there is one process I should like to mention to you; a process by which, no matter how complicated the design, no matter how minute the lines of the original, copies can be produced that shall be more completely faithful than those taken by any other means. It is the process of 'electrotyping.'"

"Ah! my young friend, it is better to leave the subject of electricity to those who have devoted time and labour to its investigation. It is a dangerous subject for the young and ignorant. I advise you not to have anything to do with it. Rash hands should never meddle with the secrets of Nature," remarked the Mystery.

"Yes, yes, it is better to shut the temple gates," said the Virgil, tauntingly; "then no one can profane the rites or [*sotto voce*] find out the ignorance of the priests."

"But it is the glory of the present day," replied the New Book, quickly, "that science does not shut up the gates of her temple, but opens them *wide*, that all who wish may enter in and worship; and her priests stand daily pointing out the vestibule to the inquiring, and are ready to explain her most sacred mysteries. But never fear, learned sir; I am not going to enter into any alarming discourse on the nature of electricity. I simply thought I should like to mention one particular way in which electricity is made to contribute to the service of the fine arts."

"We shall all be happy to listen," said the Folio, courteously.

" Electrotyping, which is one division of the art of electro-metallurgy," began the New Book, " is that of depositing metals from a solution of one or other of their salts upon a metallic or other conducting substance."

" Peste ! why, that is talking like a book with a vengeance. It's as bad as listening to the Mystery himself," said the French MS. to her neighbour. " Can't he make the thing clearer ? Let him fancy we know nothing whatever about the subject, and teach us accordingly."

" I beg pardon," said the New Book ; " allow me to begin again. You know that when a metal is united, *chemically* united, with an acid, that the substance formed by that union is called a *metallic salt*—sulphate of copper, a chemical union of copper and sulphuric acid, is an example of such a salt.

" Now you must please to bear in mind that, at the latter part of the eighteenth century and beginning of the nineteenth, the following truths were discovered by two eminent men, Professor Galvani, of Bologna, and Professor Volta, of Pavia, viz., that galvanism and ordinary electricity were one and the same thing ; that electricity could be *developed*, that is, made apparent, by *chemical* means as well as by *friction ;* and that this development of electricity could be brought about by the contact, under certain circumstances, of two dissimilar metals, such as zinc and silver, or zinc and copper. It was also discovered that by means of electricity compound substances could be decomposed and separated into the different substances of which they are composed. Now, if a compound substance, such as a *metallic salt*—sulphate of copper, for instance—is decomposed by electricity, the metal which is then separated from the acid may be deposited upon any object within its reach, say a coin or a type. To take an instance. Suppose it was a medal of which an electrotype copy was desired. It might be done in some such way as this :—A glass vessel must be nearly filled with a solution of sulphate of copper. Into this vessel place a porous porcelain tube filled with sulphuric acid up to the level of the sulphate of copper in the glass vessel. Put into the porcelain tube a thin rod formed of zinc. Fasten one end of a copper wire to the zinc rod, and the other end of the wire to the object which is to be electro-plated. Coat over every part of the medal which is not to be electro-plated with wax, and then suspend the medal in the solution of sulphate of copper. Chemical action will immediately begin; the copper will be set free from the acid and will fall, or be *deposited*, as it is termed, upon the medal. The medal thus becomes *coated* with the *metal ;* and when the process is successfully conducted, the metal is a compact substance, and receives upon its surface a perfect impression of the medal—only, of course, just the reverse way. This first coating will serve therefore as a *mould*, and the process has only to be repeated in order to produce a fac-simile of the original.

"In electrotyping from a copper plate, the first electrotype taken is, of course, *in relief*—that is, the reverse of the sunken plate. That coating will serve as a *mould* from which any number of fac-similes of the original can be produced, by a deposition of the metal."

"But I do not see what great use it can be in the art of engraving," said the French MS.

"I think you will, if you consider how extremely and minutely *accurate* the copies made by this process must of necessity be; how comparatively easy of execution it is; and how largely it can be applied—that is to say, since the notable discovery made by Mr. Robert Murray in 1840. Before that date, it was always considered that the metal deposit could only be made upon metallic substances, they being conductors of electricity, and that, therefore, no moulds could be made of any soft plastic material, such as wax or gutta-percha.

"But this gentleman discovered that the metal might be deposited on *any non-conducting* substance, provided that that substance was first coated over with black lead.

"This was a grand discovery, and has made electrotyping of double or treble the value in the arts than it was before. Wood-cuts can be multiplied by this process to any extent. The block has only to be first coated over with black lead; a mould taken in wax or gutta-percha; and from the mould, by the deposition of the metal, a fac-simile produced. It is as easy to print from an electrotype plate as from the original wood block or steel plate; and there is this additional advantage, that these electrotype plates are very much more durable than any other plates. Type is sometimes coated over with copper by this process, and rendered extremely durable."

"Most assuredly it must be," said the Great Folio. "Pray, when was electricity first applied to the purposes you have named?"

"About 1805. Brugnatelli employed galvanism for the purpose of gilding; but it was not till 1839 that Jordan, Spencer, and Jacobi showed the way in which to apply it to the higher branches of art. *Our firm* make a good deal of use of the process, and keep no less than thirteen people employed solely in that one department.

"There is another process that I think ought to be mentioned to you while we are talking about engraving; for though it is not yet largely used for the purpose of illustrating books, still it is so sometimes; and is so extensively practised in portrait and landscape taking, and as a means of multiplying copies of pictures, as to form of itself an important branch of art. I allude, of course, to the practice of photography.

"Some surprise, not to say consternation, was expressed by our learned friend the Mystery when I alluded to the subject of electricity; and I think he was rather shocked to find that we employed so grand an agent upon so trivial a matter as 'picture making.' But what will he say when he hears that the sun himself is made to contribute to men's pleasures by doing the same kind of work; in fact, that the sun is one of the cheapest and most largely patronised artists of the present day?"

"I am very sure that if Phœbus Apollo, 'the unerring lord of light,' condescends to draw for you, *he* will never miss his aim," said the Virgil, "which is more than can be said, I fancy, of other artists."

"Certainly, he is an artist that is very truthful in all he does; his lines are generally *straight*," said the New Book; "and he can never be said to flatter people. He pays no attention to the whims or vanities of those who sit to him for their portraits; nor can he even be accused of partiality—he deals with the peer exactly as he deals with the peasant. But you know even *facts* may be distorted and truth misrepresented; and these 'sun-pictures,' it must be confessed, are not always 'perfect,' nor invariably pleasant. Not through the fault of the artist, but through the want of skill and knowledge of his attendant servants, who have failed to make the proper preparations for his work, or else have not succeeded in rightly 'developing' his work when executed. And it must be admitted that the most successful photographic portraits can but give the absolute truth of a few seconds of time, and may not be, seldom are, fair representations of the prevailing characteristics of the face."

"Ah! I see; it is the fault of the palette boy who prepares the colours, if the picture is poor. A convenient doctrine that for an unskilful artist," said the French MS.

"Your ladyship is pleased to be ironical," said the Esop; "but I suspect you have overshot the mark."

"Her ladyship knows that it is next to impossible to paint well if colours are badly prepared; and that as far, therefore, as the colour is concerned, that careless 'palette boy' has helped to make an imperfect picture. But you will see what I mean by not making the needed 'preparations' for and not 'developing' the work of the sun-artist when I have explained a little some of the processes of photography.

"Photography, as our friend the Elzevir will tell you, is 'drawing by light'—at least, that is the meaning of the word itself; but the word, perhaps, is not the very best that could have been chosen for the art."

"Why not? You draw by means of the *light*; do you not? and as the word is taken from the Greek word, *phôs* (*phôtos*)—light, and *grapho*—I write, it seems to me a word well fitted for its purpose," said the Elzevir.

"The word, at any rate, must remain in office now; it is far too firmly fixed to be dislodged," replied the New Book. "The truth is, we delineate objects by *the rays of the sun;* but not by the light or the heat, strictly speaking, possessed by those rays; but by certain *chemical* properties belonging to them. We will not enter into that matter, however; it is sufficient for our purpose to know that the rays of the sun are able to effect chemical changes upon certain substances, especially upon the *salts of silver*—that is, the compounds formed by the union of silver with an acid."

"I have long been aware," said the Mystery, "that light hath a darkening influence upon *horn silver*. That fact was duly noted and commented upon, to some degree, by the wise men of my day."

"Very probably the 'horn silver' of which you speak was a mixture of silver and chlorine, called by us 'fused chloride of silver.' But though your learned alchymists of the sixteenth century noted the fact (and that was something worth the doing), they do not seem to have carried out their observations to any practical result. The great Prussian chemist Scheele seems to have been the first to take up the subject, about the year 1777, in a proper, that is, a scientific way. In 1802, our great artist in clay, Josiah Wedgwood, and Sir Humphrey Davy produced 'sun-pictures,' by coating white paper or enamelled leather with nitrate of silver, placing an engraving upon it, and exposing both to the rays of the sun. The uncovered part of the paper immediately became *black;* while the rays passing through the engraving left an image of it upon the paper underneath. But now a curious thing was noticed. The thick opaque lines of the engraving had stopped the rays from passing through, so wherever they were, the paper underneath them was *white;* while all the white places, those between the engraved lines and elsewhere, allowed the rays to go through —consequently, underneath them, the paper was *black*," said the New Book.

"So the image on the paper was exactly opposite in its black and white to the real engraving," said the Æsop.

"Exactly so. And, as a general rule, the first impression of any object taken by photography is called a 'negative,' or a reverse picture; because the light and dark parts are just reversed. A copy from the negative gives, of course, the opposite effect, and is called a 'positive,' or direct picture. But though Wedgwood and Davy had proceeded thus far, they could not find out a way to *fix* their 'sun-pictures'—that is, to prevent the light from taking any more effect upon them; so their pictures speedily disappeared by the paper becoming all black alike."

"Who, then, found out the way to keep these sun-pictures, for I conclude a way has been found to do so?" said the Great Folio.

"Some twenty or more years after these efforts of Mr. Wedgwood, two gentlemen on the continent, M.M. Daguerre and Nièpée, turned their attention to the subject, devoted much time and labour to it, and developed a very beautiful series of processes by which pictures were taken and *fixed* upon *metallic plates,* coated on one side with silver. These 'Daguerreotype' pictures are very beautiful when seen in the proper light; but if you chance to look upon the plate at a wrong angle, you may look in vain for the picture, or may see nothing but a confused smudge, which is apt to be aggravating.

"About the same time that M. Daguerre was busy on the continent with this subject, Mr. Fox Talbot was investigating it in England; and he may well be termed the Father of the Art of Photography in England, as M. Daguerre is of the art on the continent."

"Is photography a very difficult branch of art?" inquired the English MS.

"Well, one would suppose not," replied the New Book, "judging from the great number of people, young and old, who dabble in it. The fact is, photography is one of those arts that up to a certain point may be taught and learnt by rote, that is, without understanding much of the why and the wherefore. Directions can be given as to what and how things should be done, and in what proportions such and such things should be mixed; and with a moderate share of brains, and patience, and skill, certain results may be procured with tolerable accuracy. But, on the other hand, so many and so varied are the laws of optics and chemistry, on which it depends, that there is no limit to the field for research and experiment which it opens out to scientific men."

"I think it is a great pity that ignorant people are thus allowed to dabble in what is above their understanding. Surely it must tend to retard the progress of science," said the Mystery.

"O no, I do not think it does," replied the New Book. "The really scientific men of a generation will always be the real workers and true leaders in every branch of science and art. It is *they* who make the discoveries and ascertain the laws; and when they have settled a few things, they go on to find out other truths and facts. And just as an elder child leaves his discarded tools or playthings to the younger members of the family, so do they leave their discovered facts and laws; and with these the ignorant but interested lookers-on can amuse, or hurt, or instruct themselves, as the case may be, while their guides are simply pushing on to fresh fields of knowledge."

"But now as to the way of taking these sun-pictures; how is it managed?

Please to give us some idea," said the French MS.; "but do not be too learned."

"I will trouble you with as few of the details as I can," replied the New Book.

"The photographer does not need a complicated apparatus. He must, of course, have his 'camera'—that is, a dark box with a tube at one end, which can be drawn out and made longer or shorter as required, in which tube are placed one or more 'lenses.' A lens, I may perhaps be allowed to mention, is a transparent substance, generally glass, which is so shaped as to alter the direction of the rays of light which pass through it, causing thereby the objects looked at through it to appear larger or smaller, as the case may be. The glass of an ordinary eye-glass or pair of spectacles is a common example of a lens. At the other end of the camera is a ground glass screen, made movable to allow of the 'camera-slide,' a thin box or case, being put in its place. The prepared plate or paper is put into the slide, to be carried safely to and from the camera."

"I remember that the camera-obscura—literally, 'darkened chamber,'" said the Mystery, "was invented, in the sixteenth century, by that learned and clever man John Baptista Porta, born at Naples; a most truly learned mathematician and philosopher, at whose house the scientific men of the day were wont to meet for conversation and discussion on the subjects of their studies. Pity it was that the Court of Rome thought fit to put an end to those meetings."

"Why? did the learned men contrive to mix a little politics with their science?" inquired the Law Book.

"Well, it was rumoured," rejoined the Mystery, in a solemn voice, "that they discoursed of *magic* at these meetings."

"Probably they did," said the Esop. "They would be at home in that branch of learning."

"No. I assure you that it was not so; though I admit that Porta was accustomed to the predicting of events, and given to the performance of experiments that were peculiar and somewhat terrifying; and also that he wrote a treatise in Latin upon Natural 'Magic!'" replied the Mystery.

"Well, well, being in Latin, it would do the popular mind little or no

F

harm. That is one great advantage of our learned languages. Being 'dead tongues,' anybody can talk in them about anything that is considered either too bad or too good for the world in general," said the Esop, rather maliciously.

"I am afraid we hinder our young friend by our digressions, interesting though they may be," said the Great Folio, ever anxious to keep the peace.

"I was going to say," continued the New Book, "that on the glass screen at the back of the camera, the objects which are to be photographed must be first 'focussed.'"

"What do you mean by that?" asked the French MS.

"An object is said to be focussed," replied the New Book, "when the distances between the screen, the lens, and the object are so adjusted that a bright and distinct image of the object, of the required size, is formed upon the screen. Now for a word or two about the preparation of the plates or paper. The paper must be rendered 'sensitive' to the action of the light by being coated over with solutions of salts of silver. I will not trouble you with the order and different proportions of these various solutions, as, perhaps, none of us are likely to attempt to produce a 'sun-picture.' Indeed, in *this* room such a thing could not be done, for I imagine the sun never pays it a visit."

"Very true indeed," exclaimed many of the oldest inhabitants of the room.

"The paper thus prepared," resumed the New Book, "is then carried from the operating-room in the slide and placed in the camera, the shutter taken off the lens, and in a few seconds the picture is produced; not that, as a general rule, it is then *visible*; it has first to be 'developed.' The paper will require to have several solutions of salts of silver and of different acids applied to the surface with a camel's-hair brush or a piece of wool, when the picture will begin to appear and gradually grow distinct and dark. When developed the image must be 'fixed'—that is, made so that the light can have no further action upon it. To effect this, the paper must be immersed in a solution of hyposulphite of soda, which dissolves out any of the salts of silver that have remained unacted upon by the light, and then washed several times in water."

"But in this first picture I think you said that the black and white parts were just the reverse of the real object; did you not?" inquired the English MS.

"Yes; this first picture is what is called the 'negative' or reverse picture, from which it is not difficult to procure the direct or 'positive' one," replied the New Book. "To 'print' a positive from a negative, a sheet of paper must be first rendered sensitive, either by the use of a solution of ammonio-nitrate of silver or other salts of silver, or else by coating it with a film of albumen. The negative is placed downwards upon the prepared paper, and both exposed to the sun for a few minutes. When thus 'printed' the picture is 'fixed' by being in the usual manner soaked in a mixture of hyposulphite of soda and chloride of gold, and then washed several times in water. A positive print can be obtained in common writing-ink. A sheet of paper is dipped into a solution of bi-chromate of potash, and when dry exposed, under the negative, to the sun for a few minutes. The result is a brown picture upon a yellow, ground. This yellow colour can be removed by washing in water; and then, if the paper is placed in a solution of sulphate of iron, and afterwards in a strong solution of tannic acid, the salt of iron is changed into a 'tannate of iron,' and that is, as you know, common writing-ink."

"Well, these wonderful changes seem very like magic," said the French MS.

"Yes; *Nature's magic*, worked by no arbitrary caprice, but by unerring and unswerving laws, which she invites all to observe and study," replied the New Book.

"I certainly think that neither alchymist or magician, as you would perhaps term the philosophers of my day, ever produced more strange and wonderful 'transmutations' than those you have mentioned as if they were common every-day occurrences. I think many a one has been dubbed 'sorcerer,' and *treated accordingly*, in days gone by, who has not effected half the marvels that your photographers seem able to do," said the Mystery. "It is well for them they live in days of freedom."

"Indeed, I quite agree with you," replied the New Book. "'A fair field and no favour' is all that the true lover of science requires and desires. But there are just one or two things I should like to mention before we quite leave

f 2

our present subject. One is a process called the *collodion* process, so called because the glass plates used are first coated over with collodion before the 'sensitive' chemical mixtures are applied. Collodion is simply *gun-cotton dissolved* in ether and alcohol."

"But, pray, what is gun-cotton; is it used in your guns?" asked the French MS.

"Yes. It has been found that cotton, when placed in nitric and sulphuric acid, forms a compound with nitrogen, and becomes a very highly inflammable and explosive substance, more so even than gunpowder. Now, this gun-cotton, if taken and dissolved in ether and alcohol, becomes quite another thing. It is extremely adhesive; forms therefore a capital plaster, and may heal the wounds that gun-cotton perhaps has made. More wonderful changes you see. This collodion is of great use to the photographer. The glass plate is first coated over with a film of this adhesive collodion, and then placed in a bath of nitrate of silver. The image is 'developed' by means of salts of iron and acetic acid being poured over the plate. The negative is at first very faint, but is rendered darker, after it has been 'fixed,' by being dipped in a solution of cyanide of potassium. This *gradual* strengthening of a *weak negative* is said to produce excellent effects of light and shade. The plate is then varnished. In this collodion process a positive picture can be procured *at once* on the glass, by some variations in the mode of preparing the plate and conducting the processes.

"There is one process called 'photogalvanography,' invented by Mr. Paul Pretsch, manager, at one time, of the Imperial Printing Office at Vienna, which is very wonderful and beautiful, and by means of which the most elaborate engraving—one that would perhaps take two or three years to produce in the ordinary method of copper or steel engraving—can be accurately copied in about six weeks. A positive picture is first produced by photography upon a glass plate coated with *gelatin*. From that picture a mould is taken in gutta-percha, which is, of course, a *sunken* copy of the picture. Then a copper-plate matrix is procured by *electricity* from the mould, and the *plate* from which the printed engraving is to come is made by means of the electrotype process. From this plate 400 or 500 impressions can be struck. So, you see, what light and chemistry and electricity can accomplish. Engravings can, by their united aid, be multiplied to almost any extent.

"Pictures can also be taken by means of photography on copper, steel, and zinc plates, and then etched afterwards. The 'photozincography' process is of incalculable advantage to us, for by it fac-similes of national MSS. are now taken. Ancient MSS., so old as scarcely to bear handling, and which no copyist could ever hope to reproduce, are by this means preserved to us, and their treasures rendered accessible to all, because, of course, from the etched plate any number of impressions can be made."

"That must indeed be a capital use to which to apply this wonderful art," said the English MS.

"Yes indeed. I heard from one of our daily papers of one MS., among others, that has been thus quite recently made to give up its treasures, which was so old and decayed, and its leaves so stuck together with age and damp, that only a portion could be photographed."

"And what was the old MS.?" inquired the Great Folio.

"It is called the 'Silver Shrine,' a copy of the Gospels. Perhaps the oldest copy (so said the paper) existing in the world, of the fifth century, and is now in the possession of the Royal Irish Academy. It is enclosed in three cases—the inner of wood, the next of copper plated with silver, and the outside of silver plated with gold."

"It has evidently been considered a great treasure and preserved with much care," said the Quarto.

"Yes; and, according to my authority, the parts which have been photographed form part of St. Patrick's own book of private devotion," said the New Book. "You can easily imagine what immense service to the cause of literature may be thus rendered by this revivification, so to speak, of the documents recording the laws, manners, customs, religions of the past, and enabling all students of history 'to touch land for themselves,' as our Dean Stanley calls it; that is, to come in direct contact, if not with the very originals themselves, yet with the fac-similes of those ancient *written records*, without which the modern world could have had no history."

CHAPTER V.

" Now, if you will allow me, before I ask you to go with me into the press-room, I must say a little about the paper on which I was printed, and the way in which it was manufactured; for, without the paper manufacturer, I suspect there would be but few books printed, and certainly there would be no such things as ' daily papers,' " resumed the New Book.

" But there are other things that can be used, and have been used, for writing upon, before paper was known," said the French MS. " Vellum, for instance, was often and in very early times employed; was it not?"

" Most assuredly," replied the Elzevir; " for we have abundant evidence that the prepared skins of beasts were used, at least by the Jews, for writing upon. But, I suppose, there was no regular manufacture of the substance called parchment till about 200 years B.C., when Eumenes II., King of Pergamos, established it, because he could not get a supply of the papyrus paper from Egypt."

" I suppose vellum is very difficult to make, and would be far too costly for every-day wear?" said the English MS.

" Vellum, which is a fine kind of parchment, and is made from the skins of calves and kids, has certainly to go through a number of different processes before it is made fit to write upon," replied the New Book. " The skin has to be soaked, steeped, washed, placed in lime pits, in order to get rid of the fatty substances, and of the hair and wool; after which it has to be stretched and scraped, and rubbed with pumice-stone; and when all that is done, it is handed over to the parchment maker, who, with great dexterity, pares off half the thickness of the skin, leaving a smooth surface, which, after being again rubbed, is considered fit for writing upon."

" Our Saxon and Norman ancestors seem never to have used anything but parchment and vellum for their MSS. At least, I believe, none have been found upon any other material," said the English MS.

" It is a very good thing that we are not dependent upon the skins of animals for the material for our books," said the New Book. " The supply would never be found equal to the demand of the present times, I suspect."

" Nor in the earlier times of the world's history," said the Great Folio. " The Chinese, for instance, seem from a very early date to have regularly manufactured a material similar to our paper from old rags, hemp, cotton, silk, and also from the inner bark of a tree called the ' paper mulberry.' The branches of this tree, I have heard, they used to cut into lengths of about three feet, and boil them with an alkaline substance; peel off the rind; and boil it again, till it was perfectly tender, and would separate into delicate fibres. It was then placed in a pan in running water, till perfectly soft; and to make it still more fine, the pulpy mass was beaten with a wooden mallet. The soft pulp was next mixed with an infusion of rice and a particular root, and the mixed ingredients were put into a large pan. Into this pan moulds of the size of the required paper were dipped, and the sheets, when sufficiently set, placed upon a table with a piece of reed between each, and heavy weights put upon them to press out the water. The next day they were lifted out by the pieces of reed, one by one, and placed in the sun to dry." *

" The Chinese are not the only people who have found out that paper can be made from *wood pulp*. There are manufactories in America, France, Prussia, and also in our own country, where paper is produced from this material," said the New Book. " I should describe the process simply thus—a block of wood is speedily cut up into chips, and as speedily reduced to a pulp, and the pulp bleached and pressed, till it is like snow for whiteness, and like cotton for softness, and then made into paper. Indeed, it is difficult to say from what paper

* See engraving on page 17.

may not be made. Any vegetable substance that can be reduced to a liquid pulp may be made to answer the purpose."

"Then think of the large use made of the renowned Egyptian reed—the papyrus—the world-wide famous papyrus, with its soft triangular stem, and its graceful hanging plume of filaments. What treasures of thought have been committed to its keeping. From earliest days down even to the eleventh century of the Christian era, men have used it for the record of their words and deeds, their thoughts and feelings, their hopes and longings. Truly, the world owes much to the papyrus plant," said the Elzevir.

"It was very largely used in Italy, I know," said the Virgil, "and the Romans greatly improved the polish and finish of this same papyrus paper. You moderns are not the only people who can read and write, and have libraries, and so on. My master Virgil, and his friend Horace, could tell you what a literary people the Romans were in their time."

"But all the books then read must have been *written* ones," said the French MS. "Manuscripts must have been all the fashion then, however little they be thought of now."

"Yes; but the MSS. of the days of which I speak presented a very different appearance to your ladyship," replied the Virgil. "They were literally *volumes,* if you like; for, whether made of vellum or papyrus paper, they were *rolled* books. They were rolled round a stick at one end, or on two sticks, one at each end, if the MS. was a long one. At one end there was a ticket, serving the purpose of a title, called *frons,* from which comes the word 'frontispiece.' Sometimes there were two tickets, '*gemina frons.*' These MSS. were kept upright, with the labels at the top, in a cylindrical box, often made of cedar, beautifully carved, in order to preserve them from the ravages of insects. Libraries did not take up the room they do now, and had this advantage, that they could be removed easily with the owner. Then we also had our books made of more solid material," continued the Virgil, speaking as if he were really the great master himself, whose writings he preserved. "We had our *Diurni,* or day-books; our *Breviarii rationum, tabulæ accepti et expensi,* or account-books. These were books with two or more leaves of metal or iron, fastened together with rings. These leaves had a button (*umbilicus*) in the middle, to prevent them from touching each other. They were coated over with wax, and we wrote on them with an iron pen, or *stylus*, a solid sharp-pointed tool, some few inches

PAPYRUS, OR EGYPTIAN BULRUSH.

long. On the MSS. we wrote with a sharp-pointed reed (*calamus*). Certainly, we were a literary people."

"And in our Chaucer's days the 'table-book' was still in use, for he mentions—

> ' *A pairs of tables all of iverie,*
> *And a pointed polished fetouslie,*'"

said the English MS.

" I fancy I have heard that you Romans sometimes used the *stylus* for other than purely literary purposes," said the New Book.

" Well, it is true; the stylus did sometimes serve as a weapon, and ' stabbing with the pen,' I confess, was not always a mere figure of speech; but, for all that, we were a literary people," retorted the Virgil.

" Oh, no doubt; we all know that ' Cæsar was an honourable man, though Brutus says he was ambitious,' " replied the New Book, somewhat saucily.

" The Saracens," interposed the Great Folio, " it is supposed, brought from China the knowledge that paper could be *made from rags*, and established mills in Spain; and the Greeks on the Levant set up a manufacture of *cotton paper* as early as the twelfth century; and as this new paper became known to the world, the celebrated papyrus paper ceased to be employed."

" Then there was a paper mill set up at Nuremberg early in the fourteenth century," said the Esop; "that would be before the introduction of the manufacture into England, I think."

" It is true," replied the Great Folio. " There is no very reliable account of the paper manufacture in England till that published by Mr. William Caxton in 1490, a few years before his death. There were mills in England in the reign of King Henry VI., and Queen Elizabeth gave her royal patronage to the manufacture. But we are much indebted to the French refugees of 1685, who taught our people many useful things, and among them an improved way of manufacturing paper from rags; and soon after that date paper mills became common in very many parts of England."

" Yes; but all the paper made in them was made by hand; well and cleverly, no doubt, but with a great expenditure of *time* as well as labour. To make a sheet of paper out of the prepared vegetable pulp, to press and dry it ready for use, took up about three weeks' time; and now the result can be accomplished in *three minutes !*" said the New Book.

" Ah ! that would sound well in a *fable*, my friend, but hardly does for a sober narrative," said the Esop.

" Indeed, I assure you I speak no fable, but simple matter of fact; and I will very briefly show you how this marvel is accomplished," said the New

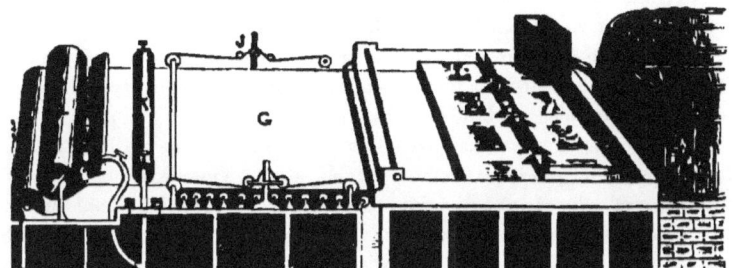

A, Stuff-Chests. c, Mixing Box. d, Sand Catches. f, Trough with Strainer Plates. G, Endless Wire Web. H, Suction Boxes. J, Pulleys carrying Deckle-strap. K, Dandy Roll. L, Couch Rolls.

M, Felt. N, Cylinders heated by Steam. O, Heavy Metal Rollers. P, Reeling Apparatus.

SECTIONAL VIEW OF PAPER-MAKING MACHINE.

Book. "But let me acknowledge that the first conception of the idea of making a continuous web of paper by machinery arose in the mind of a French workman; and that Frenchmen, at the close of the eighteenth century, first brought the idea to England. English brains and English money soon took up the idea, added to it improvement after improvement, invention after invention, till it grew to be the marvel it now is, outrivalling, in its rapidity and neatness of execution, any fabled work of fairy hands.

"Paper—what is now called paper—is, as we all know, an artificial substance produced by certain processes from vegetable fibre. This vegetable fibre, in the form of *rags* of all sorts and descriptions, has to be reduced to a liquid pulp. To do this, the rags have to be sorted, dusted, boiled, washed, beaten, bleached, tinted, and sized. All of which several operations are done by various ingenious machines, over the production of which clever men have spent the best of their thoughts and labours.

"From rags thus treated was the paper made employed in my printing. The liquid pulp to which the rags had been reduced was placed in a large vat, and made to flow gently and evenly out of a trough, on to, and over, some twelve or fifteen feet of a piece of fine *woven wire* cloth. This web of wire cloth was about thirty feet long, and was made to pass round rollers, over and over again (for which reason it is called an ' endless web ').

"On the sides of the wire cloth were large straps made of pieces of cotton gummed together, or sometimes of India-rubber. These ' deckle ' straps, as they are called, keep the liquid pulp upon the wire cloth. They can be placed near together, or farther apart, according to the required width of the paper. The wire cloth moved steadily along, and had also a slight motion given to it from side to side. As the water drained through the meshes of the wire, the vegetable fibres arranged themselves, interlaced, and became gradually felted together; a sort of natural weaving going on, in fact. In order still more to drain the water from the pulp, the web of cloth passed over ' suction boxes,' cylinders, from which, by means of air-pumps, the air had been expelled. As it did so, the water from the pulp was, of course, forced into these cylinders, to take the place of the expelled air.

"The paper pulp, considerably dried and compressed, was made to pass between two rollers called the ' couch rolls ; ' and the paper web was gently turned over from the wire cloth on to an 'endless' blanket of felt; while the wire cloth returned to receive more of the falling pulp."

1, Modern Post. 2, Modern Foolscap. 3, Old Foolscap. 4, Old Post. 5, Large-sized Papers. 6, Old Pott. 7, Modern Pott.

WATERMARKS MADE IN WRITING-PAPER.

"These terms 'deckle' and 'couch' seem familiar to me," said the Senior Defoe.

"Very likely they are," replied the New Book. "If you remember, in the process of hand-making paper, the 'deckle' was the frame laid over the liquid pulp in the wire mould, which the man held in his hand, and gently shook from side to side. And the term 'couch roll' must remind you of the 'coucher,' the man who took the mould from the hands of the first man, and turned the paper web on to the blanket bed."

"Ah, yes; I see; please to continue."

"The paper web," resumed the New Book, "was then passed, first under one pair of heavy rollers, called 'press rolls,' and then under a second pair. It was then transferred to another blanket, while the first one rolled back again to take up a fresh web. The web and the blanket were passed over heated cylinders, each one hotter than the preceding one. From the last of the heated cylinders, the dried paper passed to the cutting-machine, where it was cut into the required lengths by most ingenious machinery, which I must not stop to explain. After being cut, it was sized and pressed; and thus, in about three minutes from the time of the liquid pulp leaving the vat, was formed the continuous web of paper, part of which lies folded within my covers."

"Truly, it is very wonderful," said the Great Folio, "and beats all fable."

"Of course, paper for printing on is not so polished nor so white in colour as is writing-paper; though the printing-papers of the present day are, you will admit, wonderfully smooth and white compared to those of older date. Writing-paper goes through several processes of polishing and pressing and finishing, which need not detain us now. There are, as you all know, several sizes of printing-papers, with various names, such as foolscap, crown, demy, medium, royal, super-royal, imperial. These may be doubled or quadrupled, and are then called double foolscap, &c. I am myself printed upon double royal."

"That term 'foolscap' reminds me of the odd devices our printers used to put upon their papers, such as a fool's cap and bells, a postman's horn, a flagon. They used to sew upon the mould pieces of wire bent in the shape of these figures. You keep some of the *names*, I perceive; do the old marks still get impressed?" said the Senior Defoe.

"No; we keep the old names, but have changed the marks. Foolscap paper has a lion rampant, or Britannia; pott paper has the English arms; copy has the *fleur-de-lis.* These water-marks are only impressed upon writing-papers. They are produced by means of a roller, called the 'dandy,' made with wires placed lengthwise. Bent pieces of wire forming the name or mark are fastened on to the wires of this roll, and the roll is passed over the semi-liquid pulp. It not only impresses the mark on the paper web, but it serves to press out still more of the water, and thus still more to compress the fibres."

CHAPTER VI.

THE PRESS-ROOM.

" PERHAPS, before I begin to relate my experiences of the press-room of modern days, some of my respected friends will oblige us with their recollections of the press and press-room of other days. We shall then be the better able to notice the points of difference, and see whether the world is wiser or not than it used to be as to methods of printing," said the New Book.

" Well, I begin to suspect that you moderns would consider that we were altogether a sleepy set—compositors, readers, pressmen, printers, and publishers —in the bygone days. Not that we used to think so of ourselves, but opinions alter," said the Great Folio.

" In truth, there is not much to be said in praise of the very first sort of presses used by the earliest printers. I grant you that *they* were awkward, cumbersome things ; could only print a very little at a time ; and were hard and difficult to manage. But this earliest kind of screw-press was soon improved by a countryman of mine, one Willem Jansen Blaew, a mathematical instrument maker at Amsterdam," said the Elzevir.

" Do you mean *that* Jansen Blaew who assisted Tycho Brahe, the Danish astronomer, that strange, clever, superstitious man, who had an artificial nose of gold, said to be so well formed that no one could tell it was not his own ? " inquired the Esop.

" The same," replied the Elzevir. " One fancies the astronomer at work in his little island bestowed upon him by the Danish monarch, busy in the observatory—the one above the ground, which he called ' Uraniburg,' or City of

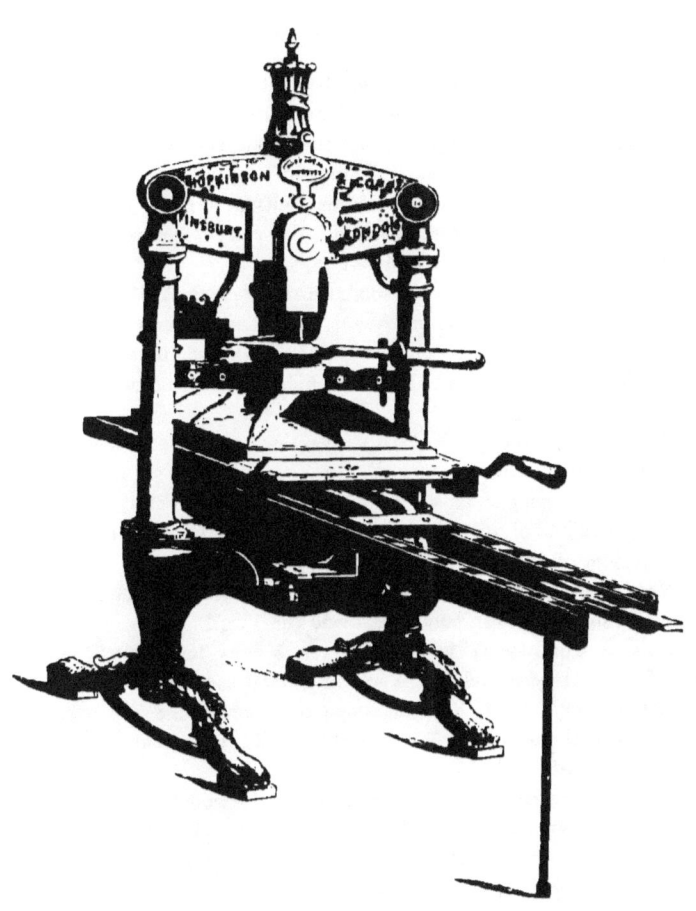

THE MODERN HAND-PRESS.

99

the Heavens; or else in the one he sunk below the ground, calling it 'Stelberg,' or City of the Stars—and our Willem Jansen Blaew with him, trying the last new instrument, or taking his instructions about the last new book or set of maps which he was going to print for him.   The improved press of Blaew's was made entirely of wood, and the 'platen' or printing surface was generally about the size of half a sheet.   Most, if not all, the present company, I expect, have passed through a press of Blaew's invention."

" A *wooden* printing-press!" exclaimed the New Book, "that must be quite a curiosity.   You must really excuse me, but I have never seen a wooden press. I have heard that there are one or two such things, in some of the oldest printing-offices; but they are either quite hidden away, or occasionally used as a hand-press for taking proofs."

" So much for the glory of past inventions, and the honour of their inventors," said the Quarto.

" Nay; the honour is not all lost," replied the Great Folio; "are not we ourselves the guardians of it?   Do we not hand down to posterity the knowledge and the memory of the men and their works?"

" Very true.   I suppose other inventions have succeeded the Blaew press, and perhaps, like his, have been laid aside," said the Virgil.

"This press of Blaew's lasted, however, a very long time," said the New Book, "for I have been told that it was in general use till about the close of the eighteenth century, when Earl Stanhope constructed one of iron, and large enough to print the whole surface of a sheet.   But even that is now considered very 'old-fashioned.'"

" Have you never seen a hand-press at work?" said the Virgil.

" O yes; I have had plenty of opportunities of seeing how they are worked, for we have, certainly, thirteen hand-presses at our place, and employ about sixteen or more people to attend to them," replied the New Book.

" Then, if you will so far oblige us, we shall be glad to listen while you describe the construction and working of a hand-press.   Our memories may be somewhat deficient as to the actual processes; and, besides, your powers of expression are certainly clearer than ours are," said the Great Folio, courteously.

"I shall be most happy to do so," replied the New Book, "and I will describe the one invented by the Earl of Stanhope, as it comes midway between the press of your Jansen Blaew and the still more modern hand-presses. The chief things to be described in the construction of the press are—the 'body' of the press, the 'platen,' the 'carriage,' the 'tympan,' and the 'frisket.' All of these names will be familiar to you.

"The 'body' of the press is a cast-iron frame, all in one piece, which is firmly fastened down to a thick piece of wood, the shape of a cross, on the ground. Attached to the body are the screws and levers, and two horizontal rails with grooves in them for the carriage. The 'carriage' is a much lighter affair than the one in the old press. The plank or carriage fits into the grooves of the horizontal rails, and is moved backwards and forwards by a spindle, and prevented from going too far by stay belts of leather, fastened underneath. The type rests upon a block of cast iron on the carriage.

"The 'platen' is a piece of cast iron, the size of a whole sheet, and is made to descend upon the type by a number of screws and levers, which are arranged upon a better plan than those in the old press of Blaew's.

"The 'tympan' is a light, square frame, with parchment stretched tightly over it, like a drum."

"Ah! *tympanum*, a drum, whence it derives its name," remarked the Virgil.

"The tympan," continued the New Book, "is fastened by hinges to the part of the carriage where the type is placed. The 'frisket,' a thin, skeleton frame (like the bars of a window without the glass), is fastened on by hinges to the headband of the tympan. The tympan takes the sheet of paper that is to be printed, and the frisket closes down upon the tympan, and keeps the sheet in its place. Now as to the way in which the press was worked, and sheets printed. There were two or three little things that required to be done before the actual sheet was printed.

"The 'inner forme' (that is, as you know, the locked-up pages of type that compose it) was brought and made fast to the cast-iron block, and the forme inked ; a sheet of stout paper fastened on to the frisket, the frisket closed over the forme, and an impression made upon that paper."

G 2

" What was the use of doing that?" inquired the English MS.

" The whole of the *printed* part on that sheet upon the frisket was cut out, and only the margin left, and that margin helped to keep the proper sheet clean. The next thing was to fold a piece of paper, so as to answer exactly to the cross-bars on the ' chase.' The chase, you remember, is the iron frame which contains the pages of type. This damp folded piece of paper was carefully laid upon the forme, the tympan closed down upon it, and an impression taken. The damp sheet clung to the tympan, and served as a guide in the after ' laying on ' of the sheet that was to be printed. Pointed wires were placed at certain places upon the tympan, which would guide the pressman when he printed the second side of the sheet.

FORME " LOCKED-UP"
AND READY FOR PRESS.'

" All these preliminaries being arranged, the pressmen were ready to begin working off the sheets. The paper had been previously well and evenly damped. The old way of doing this was to pass a part of a ream at a time through water, and then to let it soak for two or three days. But now the paper is dipped in water, and then put under heavy pressure; and in this process it only takes about two or three *hours*, instead of as many days. The moistened sheets were brought and laid upon what, in the language of the press-room, is called a ' horse.' This horse is only an inclined plane or desk, standing upon one end of a table, which table is termed a ' bank.' If the terms appear to you strange, you must please to remember they are not of my inventing. Most of them will strike you as old ones.

" A man then took a sheet from the horse, laid it upon the sheet already on the tympan, closed the frisket over it, and shut down the tympan upon the inked forme. He then ran the carriage under the platen, pulled a handle, and brought down the platen with force upon the forme. By degrees he relaxed his hold, and the platen was raised slowly upwards, by means of a balance weight;

the table was run out, the frisket and tympan raised, the sheet taken out, examined, and laid on the bank.

"All the number of impressions required of the inner forme, for the entire edition of the book, were thus worked off, and after each impression, the forme was fresh inked, by means of a large roller, formed of glue and other materials, and having two strong handles."

"But you have only printed one side of the sheets; when are you going to print the other?" asked the French MS.

BANK AND HORSE.

"As soon as the inner forme was done with, it was removed, washed with an alkaline mixture, and taken back to the composing-room. The 'outer forme' was then brought, and made fast to the block on the carriage. Before the men began to print again, a thin sheet of paper, called the 'set-off,' was put upon the tympan, in order to keep the white part of the printed sheet clean; and

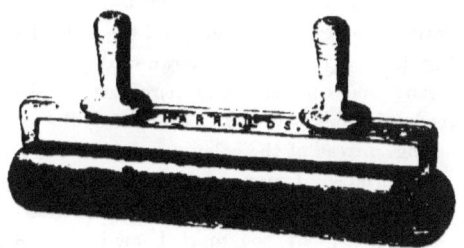

INKING-ROLLER.

as the damp ink of the printed side is apt to come off, this sheet was frequently changed. The printed sheets were then taken one by one, laid each with its printed side on to the tympan; the pressman pulled the handle, the platen descended, and each sheet was thus 'perfected,' that is, *printed on both sides.*

" You can easily understand that it is an important and difficult thing to manage, when printing the second side of the sheet, that the pages and lines shall *fall exactly over each other*, as you know they do in every properly printed book. It was in order to secure this that the pointed wires were stuck into the tympan. These wires made holes in the sheet, when the *first* side of it was printed, and when the sheet was turned, the man took care to make them pass through the *same holes* again, and thus the desired accuracy was secured, or ' perfect register,' as it is termed.

" So much for printing a book by the hand-press. Does the account recall any of your own past experiences ? "

" Yes, surely," replied the Law Book, " only as the platen of the Blaew press was smaller than the one you have described, so there were many more ' pulls' to be made by the pressman before he pulled us through."

" I think you said the press you have described is considered ' old-fashioned.' Pray, what kind of hand-press is used now ? " asked the Quarto.   " Is the difference very great ? "

" The main principle is much the same," replied the New Book ; " but a modern hand-press is altogether less cumbrous in its construction.   The wooden cross on the ground is gone, and the body of the machine stands upon its own iron legs [see page 97].   The downward pressure is produced by easier and simpler means, and can be better regulated by the pressman, and at the same time rendered more powerful.   Then, also, the platen is raised by means of a spiral spring, instead of the balance-weight of the Stanhope press."

" And so, I suppose, the pressman can get through more work in an hour than he used to do with the old press ? " said the Senior Defoe.

" True ; but you must know that in our modern printing establishments there is a giant kept that performs all kinds of work.   A giant that does our bidding with ease and regularity, when under proper guidance ; though, in unskilful hands, he may cause terrible mischief.   This giant is STEAM ; and he works our printing-presses for us, as well as other kinds, which I will presently describe.

" There is one kind of platen machine to which I must ask your attention, though only for a moment, because it is one that does a good deal of book-work in the present day. It is like a common hand-press in some respects, because it has an upright frame and a type-carriage. But instead of having *one* type-carriage it has *two*, which pass under the platen alternately. The carriages are made to pass to and fro, and the platen is made to descend and to rise by means of machinery placed underneath. There is also a special apparatus attached to each of the carriages *by which the formes are inked*. Now the machinery that accomplishes all this is worked by the giant steam; and when it is once set going, there needs no man to pull the press, no man to ink the formes. All that is required is, that there should be, at each end, a boy to 'lay on,' and a boy to 'take off,' and this machine will work off 1,000 sides, or 500 'perfected' sheets, an hour; while by the old hand-press 250 impressions, or 125 perfected sheets, was all that could be accomplished—and that could only be done when the work was not too fine, and the wood engravings were but few, and the pressmen were both clever and strong."

"It seems to me that the marvels increase as we go on," remarked the Virgil.

"So, if you please, must your power of believing," said the New Book. "Your faith must be like the fabled tent that always expanded to the size that was necessary to cover that which was placed underneath it. I have many and larger marvels to place beneath the cover of your tent; but I promise that they shall none of them exceed the bounds of truth."

"You said just now that there was no man required to ink the types," said the Law Book. "Now, though this is a wonderful age, yet, I suppose, the type does not ink itself."

"Not exactly; and yet it is true, as I told you, that in this last-mentioned machine, and in others still more wonderful—to which I will presently introduce you—the ink is not applied to the type by human fingers; that is to say, *directly* applied. You can, I dare say, recall the old method by which type was inked?"

"As well as I can remember," replied the Law Book, "it was done by means of cushions, or 'balls,' made of leather and stuffed with wool or hair. The printer used to put a layer of ink on the corner of the inking-block, then, taking a ball in each hand, he dabbed them both in the ink and then repeatedly upon the block or table, till they were evenly covered.   Then he began, and dabbed the type on the right-hand near corner; went up that side of the forme and back again, leaving off at the left-hand near corner.   He frequently turned the balls round in his hand, in order to keep them in a proper shape.   To put the ink on evenly on all parts of the forme required a great deal of care and judgment, or else when the impression was taken some parts would be pale and others too black.   A spot that printed *pale* was called a 'friar,' while one that was too black went by the name of a 'monk.'"

"Yes, that is just the way, I believe, in which type was inked in the days of Gutenberg, and one that is familiar to most in this room, I expect," said the Esop.

"The old names recall the old days, when friars and monks in flesh and blood were everywhere to be seen.   Perhaps they would now feel as strange in the streets of your modern towns as we should feel in your modern printing-offices," said the Quarto.

"Perhaps so," replied the New Book; "but what very slow work the inking with those balls must have been."

"Yes; I grant you, it was not possible to hurry over it," said the Esop.

"And besides being so slow, it must have been such uncertain work," said the New Book.

"True again, my friend; and, pray, how do you in these days remedy those acknowledged faults?" inquired the Esop.

"Very easily; by using a roller and an inking-table," replied the New Book.

"The first rollers were clothed with skin, and were the invention of Lord Stanhope.   But, in 1810, the late Mr. Robert Harrild introduced the 'composition roller.'   This 'composition,' a mixture of glue and treacle, or rather I should say, the idea of using it for inking-rollers, owes its origin to an accident which happened to a man named Edward Dyas, a printer and parish clerk in Shropshire—a man evidently with all his wits about him.   He happened to upset a glue-pot, and took up a piece of glue in a soft state, and (not having an ink-ball ready at hand) inked a forme with it, adding treacle afterwards to keep it soft.   The way in which ink-rollers are made is this: A thin rod is placed in a long iron mould, the heated and melted mixture of glue and treacle is poured into the mould, and forms a thick coating of elastic material round the rod. A curved iron bar passes over the roller, and is fastened to it, something like the iron to a garden roller, if you ever saw such a thing, and on this iron bar are two handles, that look rather like knobs drawn out and lengthened. The firm of Messrs. Harrild have gone on making improvements, and have succeeded in forming a roller *without a seam*, and in making a patent ' composition ' that is but little affected by change of climate.

" The inking-table is made either of wood or iron. At the back part of the table is a kind of trough, in which the ink is put. The ink runs down to and covers an iron cylinder which is turned by a handle, as seen in the accompanying diagram. The workman pushes his roller against this cylinder, and thus takes a small streak of ink the whole length of the roller, which is moved about the table, until it is all evenly covered with ink, and then passed over the type with a light steady motion. This is certainly a

INKING-TABLE.

great improvement upon the slow, uneven dabbing with the stuffed balls. But, in steam presses, the formes are inked by a self-acting apparatus belonging to the press, and moved by the same machinery, and that does away with the men's hands."

" Allow me to ask you one question before we go any further," said the Quarto. " You speak of the great improvement in the method of *inking* the type; may I ask if you have made equal improvement in the *ink* itself? Judging from the appearance of the Senior Defoe, and others of my junior neighbours, it would seem to me that the ink used in *their* days had certainly deteriorated from that used in my day, and that of my friend the Esop. I think, without being accused of the vanity and partiality of age, I may say that my black letter had far better ink laid upon it than was ever placed upon their more modern and fashionable type."

"Most assuredly you may, for none can gainsay you," replied the New Book. "Your ink is far more rich and black than the ink of your descendants. Your pages in that respect have a look of vigour in them far greater than I can hope that mine will show, if I should even exist for so long a time as you have done. Decidedly, the early printers must have known how to make splendid ink."

"It is said that Fust and Schœffer first introduced *black* ink," remarked the Esop. "The ink used in the 'Biblia Pauperum' was *brown*. But, certainly, our ink was very good. You have not beat us there as yet."

"The Romans, Pliny says, made their ink from soot taken from the furnaces, but some they prepared from the cuttle-fish," said the Virgil. "I dare say you know they used two kinds, red and black; the red was prepared from cinnabar."

"I suppose ink is much about the same kind of thing, whether it is used for writing or for printing?" said the French MS.

"No; there is a considerable difference in the two kinds of ink used for the different purposes. Ink used for writing must be *gummy*, while that for printing requires to be *oily*. The qualities most needed in a good ink for printing are— that it should not flow too easily; that it should adhere well; and that it should dry quickly when in layers, but not when in the lump. The ink is made of lamp- black and linseed-oil, well boiled, and even burned. A little turpentine is some- times added to help the drying power. Vermilion is used in the red ink of printers. In the ink prepared for copper-plate printing, the oil is not boiled so much, and is not so sticky as printers' ink, and consequently it both flows more freely into the lines, and can be wiped off with more ease. And the carbon used is what is called 'Frankfort black,' which is a charcoal said to be made from vine twigs. This is softer and less gritty than lamp-black," replied the New Book.

"What is lamp-black?" inquired the French MS. "I have no doubt, it is very ignorant of me not to know. I have an idea, of course; but I would like to be told in so many words."

"The term lamp-black is given to that fine soot which is formed when oily substances, and substances which contain bitumen, are burned in a particular way. This charcoal from oils is a light, powdery substance; soot is simply charcoal, or carbon, deposited from an oily substance."

"Thank you," said the French MS. "Now please to say what *writing-ink* is made from, such as has been used upon my pages."

"Writing-ink is made from a mixture of galls, alum, gum, and a salt of iron," replied the New Book. "Red ink, for writing, is made of Brazil wood, gum, and alum."

"Our Saxon ancestors must have known how to make good lasting *black writing-ink*," said the English MS. "I doubt whether any can be made in these days to match it for beauty and durability."

"Our French neighbours, I believe, make excellent ink," replied the New Book. "And we English can and do also make very good ink, and use it with all the better class of books. There are, of course, inferior kinds made—most unwisely, in my opinion. The poor ink is often used for the sake of cheapness, in getting up books for the millions that now read them. Our common ink is not, perhaps, so durable as could be wished; but it *flows* exceedingly well; and it is fortunate for our authors and writers that it does so—when the ink will not flow, the thoughts are apt to lag behind."

"Ah! ah!" exclaimed the Virgil. "There was a clever young poet, named Persius, who lived in the days when my master lived, and he describes a lazy young student blaming his *writing material* for his own idleness. I would not insinuate, for a moment, that any of the writers of the present day, young or old, ever unjustly blame their materials."

"Oh, no—of course not," replied the New Book, merrily.

CHAPTER VII.

THE MACHINE-ROOM.

" AND now I wish, if possible, to set open the doors of one of the large press-rooms in a modern printing establishment, that you may enter in, and contrast the *old* and the *new*," said the New Book; " but I feel how unequal my powers of description are to effect the purpose I desire.

" In the solitude and silence in which you have passed so much of the latter part of your lives, it must be difficult to you to understand the ways and doings, the hurry and turmoil, the business and pleasures of the world, as it is in the present day. And if, by the aid of memory, you transport yourselves to the scenes of your early youth, and recall the time when you were yourselves ' passing through the press;' yet even that, I fear, will help you but little (except by way of contrast) to form a right conception of the interior of a press-room of these modern days."

" Never mind, my young friend," said the Great Folio, encouragingly; " we will do our best to follow where you lead."

" The size of the room, the noise and the heat," continued the New Book; " the mass of men and machinery collected together in it; the large, strange, complicated machines, so unlike those you remember, as to make it seem impossible that they can be printing-machines; the constant whirr of the innumerable wheels; the rotation of the cylinders; the clanking of the type-carriages; the ceaseless *thud, thud*, of the unseen steam-engines—the giant hands that set and keep in motion the whole mass of machinery, from the largest to the smallest detail of the wheels and springs—that giant power, resistless in its force, relentless in its regularity, yet apparently so easy to manage that a child's hands may stop or set it going. All this and other things combined make the interior of a modern press-room, to an unaccustomed eye, a scene of almost painful bewilderment. But, by degrees, the confusion disappears, and both men and machines are discovered to be marshalled by order and controlled by intelligence.

"Now I must try and give you some idea of the machine, and the processes by which I myself became a *printed book*.

CYLINDER PRINTING-MACHINE.

"The Cylinder Printing Machine, much used in the present day, consists of a large cast-iron frame, about fifteen feet long, and five feet broad; and upon this frame are fastened all the different parts of the machine. The four cylinders, the carriage, and the inking apparatus are the chief things to be noticed.

"That which would, perhaps, strike you the most, from the unlikeness to anything in the old presses, would be the two large 'printing cylinders.' These cylinders are each about nine feet in circumference, and are placed about two feet distant from each other. The axes of these cylinders are fastened into upright supports attached to the frame of the machine. About two feet of the circumference of each of these printing cylinders are covered with a blanket of fine woollen cloth.   Between these two printing cylinders, and raised a little way above them, are placed two smaller cylinders, generally spoken of as 'drums.' The use of these you will see presently.

"Underneath these printing cylinders is the type-carriage, which runs backwards and forwards from one end of the frame to the other, upon rollers, which run in grooves.   At each end of this type-carriage is arranged the apparatus for *inking the type*.   This inking apparatus consists of a 'metal trough,' in which the ink is put; a 'ductor roller,' which is made slowly to revolve, and take up a thin film of ink from the trough ; an 'elastic roller,' which is so hung that it knocks against the ductor, takes ink from it, descends and dabs the ink down upon that part of the type-carriage termed the inking-table ; 'distributing rollers,' which are placed rather obliquely across the carriage, and gently roll and *distribute* the ink upon the table ; and, lastly, the 'inking rollers,' which, as the carriage moves to and fro, take up the ink on the table, and roll it over the formes.

"Now, if all this explanation is as clear as I desire, we can begin to print."

"Stop one minute, if you please," said the Elzevir; "I must try to connect all these new ideas of your grand machine with those that have already been impressed upon my mind; and I must connect them either by their points of resemblance or their points of difference."

"And a very good way it is of binding together knowledge and ideas ; in fact, I suspect it is the only way in which the mind can build up its images," said the Quarto.

"Very well.   There is the type-carriage, which will, I suppose, be 'run in and out,' with the type upon it," resumed the Elzevir.

"There are these two large cylinders, which, I suppose, are to do the *pressure* part of the business; two other small cylinders, whose work we have not yet learnt; and a set of rollers, which stand in the place, and do the work of, the balls and slab of other days, and ink the formes.   Now, if I am right, we shall be happy to proceed."

"Perfectly right, so far," replied the New Book.

"There are just two things, points of *difference*, which I wish you to impress upon your minds before we go on. First, that in this machine the paper is not laid upon the *type*, but upon the surface which produces the pressure. Secondly, that the pressure is *not* produced by a *flat surface* descending upon the formes of type, but by the rotatory motion of cylinders.

"Now you will remember that after the necessary 'corrections' had been made by the compositor, and the 'revises' examined, the 'formes' were pronounced to be 'ready for press.' The heavy formes were placed in a long iron trough-like carriage, mounted on two low wheels, and conveyed to a steam lift, which descended with them to the machine-room.

"The *inner* forme was laid at one end of the type-table; the *outer* forme at the other end. The sheets of blank paper, duly moistened, were laid on a table at one end of the machine, the one where the *inner* forme had been placed. By this table, on a raised platform, stood a boy, called the 'layer-on.' This boy took a sheet of blank paper,

FORME-CARRIAGE.

and placed it upon a flat surface called the 'feeder.' Before we go further, I must tell you that along this feeder, and round all the cylinders, there are a number of flat girths, or tapes, half an inch broad. These tapes are so arranged that they fall upon the margins of the sheet, and between the pages of the type. By these 'endless' bands, or tapes (endless because they go round and round, and act over and over again), the sheet of paper laid upon the feeder was delivered on to the first of the large printing cylinders. The cylinder and paper began to turn round, the type-table moved, the inking-rollers passed over the type, and the cylinder met the inner forme at exactly the right moment, and the blank sheet was *printed*. The first cylinder still turned, and the sheet, guided by the tapes, was passed *over* the first of the small cylinders, or 'drums,' *under* the other, and then on to the second large printing cylinder. This second cylinder revolved, and brought the *unprinted* side of the sheet just exactly in time to meet the *outer* forme, which the movement of the carriage brought up, ready inked by the rollers, against it; and thus the *second side* of the sheet was printed. As the second cylinder continued its revolution, the printed sheet was deposited on the space, or table, between the two printing cylinders, from whence a boy, the 'taker-off,' took it off, and laid it down in front of him. Thus sheet after sheet was printed, as fast, in fact, as the layer-on and taker-off could move their fingers. · You see, the beauty of this machine is, that it *perfects* the sheets—that is, it prints the two sides of the sheet without its being removed from the machine, and thus produces 'perfect register.' If you have followed me, and if I have expressed the thing clearly, you will have perceived that the sheet became completely *turned over* during its journey, and that the *printed side* was laid upon the blanket of the second cylinder. The use of the two smaller cylinders, or 'drums,' was simply to help the passage of the sheet from the first to the second printing cylinder, and to turn it over properly and smoothly."

"Well, it is very, very wonderful, I must admit," said the Elzevir; "but how does it happen that the type meets the cylinders at exactly the right time and place?"

"The movements of the machine are so contrived that the type-carriage is made to go and return to the same place during the time that the cylinders make one entire revolution. The horizontal motion of the carriage and the rotatory one of the cylinders are thus made to 'reciprocate,' or answer to each other. You must also bear in mind that each forme gets touched by the ink-rollers eight times for each impression; that the feeder must supply a *blank* sheet once during every revolution of the large wheel; and that about 1,500 impressions are printed in one hour."

"And, pray, what moves the large wheel, who turns the cylinders, and who pulls the carriage?" said the Senior Defoe.

"The machine is connected by a band, or strap, with a steam-engine, and the strap can be easily altered, and the machine stopped in a minute. That steam-engine causes the machine to perform every movement, except the 'laying on' and the 'taking off' of the sheets, which, as I said, were done by the two boys. Compare all this with the 125 sheets an hour of one-fourth the size worked by the two men with the old hand-press, and give us moderns the credit of having made some considerable alterations in the methods of printing. Surely I may call the alterations *improvements*," said the New Book, exultingly.

"Most assuredly," exclaimed several of the old Books.

"Every one must admit that the term is very justly applied," said the Elzevir.

"May I ask if you have more than one of these wonderful machines at the establishment from whence you issued?" inquired the Quarto.

"O dear, yes; we have certainly not less than one-and-twenty of these cylinder, besides five platen machines."

"And does one steam-engine work them all?" inquired the Great Folio.

"No, though it might do so; but we have three steam-engines of twenty horse-power each," replied the New Book, not without a sort of personal pride in the resources of his establishment.

"Pray, how long have these cylinder machines been in use?" inquired the Senior Defoe; "and who was the clever inventor?"

"This machine," replied the New Book, "is, like every other machine, the result of its immediate predecessors; and the history of one such machine necessitates the mention, at least, of other previous ones. In 1790, a Mr. William Nicholson formed the idea of using a cylinder, instead of a flat surface pressure, and of attaching an inking apparatus to the machine itself. In his design, I believe the type was fixed upon a cylinder which revolved against another cylinder, covered with soft leather, and the paper was placed between the two cylinders. But his plan was never thoroughly worked out. A German, Mr. König, has the honour of being, in 1804, the first to apply *steam* power to printing. He also carried out still further the main idea of Mr. Nicholson's, as to cylinder printing—with this difference, that the type was placed upon a flat surface, and the paper on the cylinder. Mr. Walter, the enterprising proprietor of the *Times*, entered into arrangements with Mr. König, and after ten years' labour, on the 28th November, 1814, was issued the first number of the *Times* that was printed by machinery worked by the aid of *steam*. That date marks the

H

commencement of a new era in the history of printing, second only in importance to the introduction of the art itself. Then, in 1818, Messrs. Applegath and Cowper improved upon Mr. König's machine, and brought it to the perfection I have tried to describe."

" So, thus, one thought gets built on to another thought," remarked the Great Folio. " First came the idea of using the cylinder, instead of the *flat* surface pressure; then the thought of making steam move the machinery; and then this complete and wonderful machine which you have described to us."

" Yes; and there are yet more wonderful ones still, to which I shall hope to introduce you before we part company," said the New Book. " But there are one or two things to which I must first allude.

" To return to the printed sheets. From the press-room, they were taken to the drying-room, and after hanging for some time to get thoroughly dry, they were put between boards, and placed in an hydraulic-press, and 'hot-pressed.'"

" Pray, what kind of a press can that be? " inquired the French MS.

" An hydraulic, or hydrostatic press, is a press constituted on one of the principal laws in the science of hydrodynamics."

" Worse and worse," exclaimed the French MS. " Excuse me, but one hard word does not explain another—at least not to my weak mind."

" Nor to any mind," replied the New Book; " but both hydrostatics and hydrodynamics are words which carry their meaning about with them, as you see when you take them to pieces, which I will, with your leave, do at once. The first comes from the Greek, *hudor*—water, and *statis*—standing still; and means the science which treats of the laws, or rather the *facts* discovered about water, when in a state of *rest*. And the other, hydrodynamics, comes from *hudor* —water, and *dunamis*—force or power; and relates to the laws or facts regarding water, when in a state of *motion*.

" An hydraulic-press is a long upright frame, of four posts, a top, and a movable iron plate, on which are placed the things that are to be pressed. Underneath this plate is an iron piston, or 'ram,' that fits into a large massive cylinder, and can be moved up and down in it. Near to the press stands a pump, sometimes two, over a reservoir of water, and a narrow tube connects the press and the pump. The sheets were laid on the iron plate of the press; water was raised from the reservoir by the pump, forced along the narrow tube into the cylinder of the press, and by that, the large piston and the iron plate, and its burden of sheets, were all raised, and the sheets most powerfully pressed."

HYDRAULIC-PRESS.

"Do you really mean to say that the water pumped into the press was really able to raise all that weight: how is it possible?" said the Esop, incredulously.

"I mean exactly what I say," replied the New Book. "And the reason of it lies in this one particular fact respecting water, which is, that its particles transmit, or send, to take the commoner word, any pressure that is put upon them, at any one part, *equally* and *freely* in *every direction*. In this case, for instance,

H 2

the small piston of the pump put a certain amount of pressure on the water which it forced into the cylinder of the press; and that water carried that same amount of pressure to *every part* of the *end* of the *large* piston in the cylinder. Now, as the piston belonging to the press is much larger than the piston of the pump, there was, of course, a much greater quantity of power exerted on the end of the large piston of the press than was exerted by the end of the smaller piston of the pump. Of course, the amount of force exerted on the end of the large piston depends upon the proportion which its diameter bears to the diameter of the small piston. You must, however, always remember that the small piston has to move a long distance, or to make a number of strokes up and down, in order to move the great piston a small distance.

"Now, perhaps, you can form an idea of the way in which a small power can be multiplied to a great extent, and a little weight sustain or raise a much larger one."

"But I think you said that your printed sheets were *hot-pressed*. How was that effected?" said the English MS.

"Well, it is hot work enough, I assure you," replied the New Book, "to be subjected to the heavy pressure of an hydraulic press; but the *hot* pressing part of the business is effected by means of steam, by which the iron plate becomes heated.

"I think I mentioned, when we were in the press-room, going through the processes of the hand-press, that the 'formes,' when done with, were washed with an alkaline mixture, taken to the 'composing-room,' and there 'distributed'—that is, the type was broken up, and each letter put into its proper division in the compositor's case. It is astonishing how quickly this can be done. The man holds a handful of type in his left hand, takes a word or two between the finger and thumb of his right hand, and drops the different letters into their different places. A quick compositor can distribute 50,000 letters in a day.

"But, now, what will you say to a *machine* 'composing' and 'distributing?'"

"Why, I say that men will some day be pushed out of the way by their own machines, and be of no use at all," said the Mystery.

"Exactly so, of no use at all, except to *invent* them," said the Esop. "But are you serious as to a *machine* doing this kind of work?"

" Perfectly so," replied the New Book.

" The machine that I am going to describe very briefly can, when once fairly set off, pick out the right letters, compose them into words, *arrange the* *spaces*, and also, if required, distribute the letters afterwards ; and do all this at a very much quicker rate than any human fingers can accomplish."

" We await the explanation of your words with curiosity," said the Quarto, in its driest possible manner; " at present, you will excuse my saying so, they strike me as extravagant, not to say ridiculous."

" I must hasten to do the ' justification ' of my words," said the New Book, unmoved by the severity of the Black-lettered Quarto's remarks.

" There have been several machines constructed for the purposes of ' composing ' and ' distributing.' But, though ingenious and complicated in principle and detail, they have not been found so useful, nor met with that general acceptance, which their inventors expected and desired. The one I particularly wish to introduce to you has been in working operation in London, the north of England, and in Edinburgh, for some time, and may, therefore, to a very great extent, be pronounced a success. The machine consists of two entirely distinct parts ; in fact, properly speaking, there are two machines. The first is a small affair, comparatively speaking, and resembles a piano in some degree, as it has a key-board with fourteen keys. Now, if you knew anything about the Jacquard loom cards used in the process of weaving, you would be struck with the clever adaptation made in this machine of the principle of those cards. The fourteen keys of the key-board are connected with fourteen *pins;* each key when it is struck moves a *pin*, and the pin when moved pierces a hole in a long strip of paper arranged for the purpose. These pins make holes in different positions along certain lines on the paper ; and according to the *position of the hole in the* *paper*, it represents either one letter or another of the alphabet. Thus the letters and words of the ' copy ' are pricked out upon the paper by the *pins;* the pins are moved by the keys; and the keys are moved, I admit, by human fingers guided by human brains."

" Ah, I thought you would be obliged to have human agency in the affair," said the Quarto.

"Never meant for a moment that we should be without it altogether, my dear sir," replied the New Book. "To say nothing of the inventor himself, the person or power that strikes these keys belongs, most assuredly, to the race of mankind. Now, though none of us in this room can be supposed to have much practical acquaintance with the keys of a piano, yet we can perceive that ten keys could be struck with very much greater rapidity than ten letters could be picked out of their several divisions, and placed in the 'composing-stick,' let the compositor be as dexterous as it is possible to be."

"Yes, that must certainly be granted by every one," said the Great Folio.

"Very good; let us now take another step," said the New Book. "This *perforated* paper is taken, in the next place, to the 'composing-machine.' I will not enter into the details of this machine; but I think I may be able to give you some idea of the principal features of it. You must please to think of twenty boxes, or pockets, with seven divisions in each box for letters. These letter-boxes, or 'type-pockets,' are arranged round a wheel-like machine. (You must think of a wheel lying horizontally, not of one placed in an upright position.) Against and opposite to each box there stands a piece of machinery, called by the most appropriate of names, a 'pickpocket.' Each of these twenty pickpockets has seven fingers, or hooks. Fastened to these pickpockets and their seven fingers are different levers and triggers. Now, when these levers and triggers are moved, each pickpocket picks out, with the finger or fingers that are pulled, the letter or the letters in the divisions of the type-pocket against which it stands."

"Very good; very good indeed," said the Law Book. "But who is to move the pickpockets and their clever fingers? It strikes me you will want a man for each pickpocket, and that will be worse than your one man compositor."

"Wait a minute," replied the New Book. "You will find that the only compositor at work in this machine is the piece of perforated paper I before described. This perforated paper is made to pass over a small cylinder, which cylinder is also pierced with holes. Above this cylinder are arranged *fourteen pins;* these pins are attached to a number of levers and triggers. As the perforated paper passes over the cylinder, some of the holes must be brought in contact with some of the pins. When the holes in the paper and the pins are opposite each other, then the pins enter the holes in the paper, and the holes in the cylinder, and as they do so, they touch some of the levers and triggers belonging to the pickpockets; and thus the pickpockets get out of their boxes the required letters. The letters drop into a groove, and are pushed along by mechanical means, till they come to an inclined plane, when another properly directed push sends them down into the 'composing-stick.' 'Justification,' or the arranging of the spaces, is done with this machine by means of the 'perforations,' which gives it a great advantage over the other composing-machines, as with them the 'justification' of the composed matter had to be done *afterwards*, by hand. The work of 'distribution' can also be performed by this machine, by a somewhat similar process; but it is at present found to be cheaper to distribute type by means of girls, rather than machinery. Now, when I add that this composing-machine, worked by steam, can pick out and set up 15,300 letters an hour, and is equal to the work of ten clever men, I think you will all allow that I have not boasted in vain, and that I have, as I promised to do, '*justified my words.*'"

Most unqualified assent was given by every one of the Books.

"I must beg to retract my epithets," said the Quarto; "*they*, at any rate, have not been 'justified.' Our young friend will know how to pardon the incredulity of age. I should like to know at what rate the holes in the paper can be pierced."

"The perforations," replied the New Book, "can be done at the rate of eight or ten thousand an hour; and the great beauty of the plan is, that the perforations can be done by almost any one, with a little pains-taking, and away from the office, so that authors can, if they like, prepare their own paper for the machine. The drilled paper can be used again, at any time, for other editions, and it will do also for any type, and any similar machine. Altogether, it struck me, when I heard about it, as being a very ingenious and beautiful contrivance."

"It is most wonderful, and, were it not from *good authority*, would be almost incredible. Pray, who may claim the credit of this singularly clever invention?" said the Great Folio.

"Mr. Alexander Mackie, of Warrington, proprietor of the *Warrington Guardian*, is the successful inventor," replied the New Book.

NEWSPAPER PRINTING-MACHINE.

CHAPTER VIII.

THE NEWSPAPER PRESS.

" I HOPE you are now prepared to unfold your tent of belief to a very considerable extent; for I have a few rather large and surprising things to place beneath it," remarked the New Book.

" It seems to me that we have already stretched our power of credence almost to its very uttermost," said the Quarto.

" Yes, we have heard of greater marvels than our master, Defoe, himself could have possibly imagined; and, you know, he is considered great in matters of *fiction*," said the Senior Defoe.

" Truth is often stranger far than fiction," returned the New Book; " not that that is an original remark, by any means; but it is one, the truth of which every day confirms, and to which I am sure you will all assent when I have finished my present history."

" I suppose you are not going to call the cylinder machine for printing, which you have last described, ' old-fashioned;' and tell us it is now put away in some out-of-the-way corner, together with the *wooden* presses, seeing that you yourself were printed by it, and that so very recently?" said the Elzevir.

" No, I am certainly not going to say that *that* machine is laid aside, for we have, as I said before, at least twenty-one in daily use at our establishment. But though that machine is very largely employed in *book* printing, I am going to show you that it is quite unequal, wonderful as it confessedly is, to supply the wants of the newspaper-reading public.

"'The printing-machine I described has, if you remember, *two* printing cylinders, and is able to *perfect* the sheets, print them on both sides, thus securing most 'perfect register.' But in newspaper printing, it is not so absolutely essential that there should be this perfect register. *Speed* is the grand thing aimed at; though, as you will see by-and-by, *register* and other things have been secured as well as *speed*. This cylinder machine was invented about 1818. In 1827, Messrs. Applegath and Cowper devised a machine on a similar plan, but with four printing cylinders, four boys to lay on, and four boys to take off; that was two boys to each cylinder. By it they were able to turn off about 6,000 *impressions* (not perfected sheets) an hour. But this 6,000 an hour was not found sufficient; and, in 1848, Mr. Augustus Applegath determined to try an entirely new principle.

"You remember I told you that the formes, and the inking-table, and all the inking-rollers were arranged on a flat, horizontal surface, which was moved back and forwards; while the paper *rotated* on a cylinder. Now Mr. Applegath resolved that the type and the inking apparatus should be also made to *revolve* as well as the paper."

"What advantage was there to be gained in doing that?" asked the Elzevir.

"Well, you see, that in the moving the type-carriage to and fro, there is always a little time and labour lost in the reversing the motion. In this machine of Mr. Applegath's there was a large centre vertical cylinder of cast iron, 64 inches in diameter, and 200 inches in circumference. This large cylinder was surrounded by eight small cylinders, only forty inches in circumference. On the eight small cylinders the paper was placed; on the large central one, the forme of type and the inking apparatus were arranged."

"But how could the type, the forme, be fastened on to a round surface? You cannot surely bend the heavy 'chase,' with the 'furniture' and the type?" said the Esop.

"No, you cannot curve the formes of type," replied the New Book, "that is quite true. But a plate of iron can be curved, and a plate *was* curved to suit the cylinder—the part of it, at least, on which the type was placed. On this *curved* plate the formes of type were built up, so as to make the sides of a polygon. The type was made fast by the aid of the 'column rules,' as they are called—the long strips of brass which print the lines seen between the columns of print in a newspaper,—and the 'chases' were well secured on to the iron plate."

" But how could the ink and the inking-rollers act on this upright cylinder?" inquired the Esop.

" You shall see," replied the New Book. "Opposite to that part of the cylinder on which the type was placed, is the part which answers to the 'inking-table' of the horizontal type-carriage. The ink was kept in a reservoir above the machine, and was spread upon the inking-table by means of the 'ductor' and the ' vibrating rollers,' while others, the 'inking-rollers,' spread it over the type. As I said, there are eight printing cylinders standing round the larger cylinder, so there are eight sets of rollers, one set for each cylinder."

" You say there are eight printing cylinders; then has each of the eight a sheet of paper on it ready to be printed?" asked the English MS.

" Yes; each of the eight printing cylinders has its own sheet, and the sheet is applied to the cylinder in a complicated but ingenious manner. Near to each of the printing cylinders is a sloping desk, with a number of the large newspaper sheets on it. By the side of each desk stands a boy, who lays a sheet so that a set of hooks can take hold of it and draw it down an upright frame, on which are a number of tapes; the sheet then gets moved into an horizontal direction, and is guided by other tapes till it is applied to the cylinder. Each of the eight cylinders is made to turn round in exactly the same time as the large one. So, when the large cylinder turns, the ink-rollers take the ink, distribute it on the inking-table, the inking-rollers roll it over the type, the type presses against each of the eight cylinders in turn, and the eight different sheets get printed on *one side*. As each sheet is printed, it is guided by tapes along the other side, first of the horizontal frame, and then of the upright frame, till it reaches another desk, when a boy, the ' taker-off,' lays hold of it and places it on a heap. Of course, there are wheels and screws and levers innumerable by which all these different movements are effected, and of which I could not if I would, and would not if I could, trouble you with an explanation. I hope you will be able to form some idea of the main features of this clever *vertical* printing-machine."

"Thank you," replied the Great Folio. "The fault is *ours*, not yours, if we fail to do so. It seems a very ingenious machine, and the eight printing cylinders with the eight sheets must get through a great deal of work. Pray, how many impressions can be turned off in an hour by this machine ? "

"The number, as you will easily understand, must chiefly depend on two things—the rate at which the central cylinder is made to revolve, and the speed with which the 'layers-on' can feed the smaller cylinders. Suppose they feed at the rate of twenty-five sheets a minute, and the cylinders turn at the rate of twenty-five revolutions to the minute, then the eight printing cylinders, together, will turn off 12,000 impressions every hour," replied the New Book; "pretty well that for one machine, is it not ? "

"I think so, indeed," said the French MS. "The world ought to be well content with that."

"But the world was not content; the demand for newspaper reading kept increasing and increasing, and the question was how to meet the demand."

"It seems to me easy enough," said the French MS. "The printers, —proprietors rather, I should say—would require to have a greater number of machines; if one did not print enough, why, have more, that's all."

"That is very easily thought and said, your ladyship," replied the New Book; "but if you belonged to a printing establishment, you would find the question not quite so easily settled.

"The making, setting up, and working of large machines cost a tremendous amount of time and labour and money; and the question to be answered is, not whether such and such a number of machines can or cannot work off a certain amount of work, but by what methods the required work can be performed so as to use *the least* of those three precious things—time, labour, and money. So clever brains went on still inventing; and Messrs. Hoe and Co., of New York, introduced to the printing world another form of machine, in which the axis of the centre cylinder is placed *horizontally*, instead of being upright as in Mr. Applegath's. The printing cylinders by which it is surrounded are also horizontal.

"The type is fastened to the centre cylinder, and takes up about a quarter of the surface. The remainder of the surface is occupied with the inking apparatus.

"In this machine, the ink is supplied from a reservoir beneath it. As the large cylinder revolves, the inking-rollers rise up, ink the forme, and sink back on to the 'distributing' surface of the cylinder, which is lower than the forme of type. Then the type is carried to each of the printing cylinders, with the sheets upon them, and each sheet is printed on *one side*. The sheets are placed on the cylinders by human fingers, there being a boy stationed by each printing cylinder. But they are 'taken off' by *machinery*."

"Ah, so you get rid of the 'takers-off' in this machine; I suppose, presently, you will do without the 'layers-on.' I am getting prepared for anything," said the Esop, half-cynically.

"Now, suppose there are *ten* printing cylinders," continued the New Book, "and that the machine makes thirty-four revolutions in a minute, and that each 'layer-on' can do so at the rate of thirty-four sheets a minute; you can easily see how many impressions this machine can work off in an hour."

"Yes; it will turn off 340 impressions a minute, that will be 20,400 an hour," said the Law Book.

"I understand that the boys in New York move their fingers faster than our English boys can; for they are found able to *lay on* as many as forty-two sheets a minute," said the New Book. "Now it is easy to make the machine revolve at the same rate, so that $42 \times 60 \times 10 = 25,200$ impressions an hour can be turned off. But, as a general rule, in England, thirty or thirty-two sheets a minute is found to be the quickest rate at which they can be properly and smoothly laid on.

"And now, if you will allow me, I should like to mention one or two facts about the printing of the *Times* newspaper. I select that particular paper, because I believe it has been the leader in the art of printing, as applied to newspapers. I think you will then be able the more clearly to see what *had already been done*, and what *remained to be accomplished*, if accomplishment were possible. You will remember, I dare say, that I told you that on November 24th, 1814, the *Times* newspaper was printed by machinery moved *by steam*; the first paper that had ever been so printed. All honour to Mr. König, who first introduced the idea, and to Mr. Walter, proprietor of the *Times*, who first carried it out. The step thus taken was of incalculable importance, and the progress in printing from that time was sure and rapid.

"In May of 1850, the *Times* and its supplement consisted of 17,000 lines, made up of 1,000,000 pieces of type. This immense quantity of matter was set up, and in about four hours from the time it was sent to press 30,000 perfect copies were printed."

"What a tremendous number of copies, and of one newspaper alone; but, perhaps, that was only an occasional number," said the Great Folio.

"O no; it is by no means exceptionally great. Two years later, on the 14th November, the day after the funeral of the great Duke of Wellington, 70,000 copies were printed, and those were all done by two of Applegath's vertical machines, such as I have described."

"I wonder where all the readers are to be found. It would have been difficult to find so many, the world over, when I was written, I suspect," said the French MS.

"Oh, you know that now, in England, no gentleman thinks of beginning his breakfast without his daily paper; if by chance it should fail him, his cook and his wife are sure to taste of his displeasure. And the poor man, as well as the rich man, will now have, if possible, his paper, of some kind or other," replied the New Book. "But we must go on, and still on, in our history of progress. You have all heard, I dare say, of the Crimean War. It may, possibly, have seemed a somewhat short and tame affair to some of you, who remember the long protracted wars of earlier days; but to the people then living, I believe, from all I have heard, that it was a time of great excitement. Every one was wanting the 'latest news' of the war, and so great was the demand for papers, that it was found impossible to get all the copies of the *Times* that were ordered printed before nine or ten o'clock in the morning. That was far too late to suit our business gentlemen.

"So Mr. Walter and his associates pondered over the ways and means by which the difficulty could be overcome. The papier-maché process for getting moulds from the type had just been discovered, and it occurred to Mr. Walter that if he could take more than one *cast from the same mould*, there would be a great advantage gained."

"In what way?" asked the English MS.

"Because more than one machine could be printing the same page at the same time, I should suppose," said the Elzevir.

"Just so," replied the New Book; "and that was something gained.

"But, as I think I mentioned when we were talking about stereotyping, Mr. Walter and his assistants went on making experiment after experiment, and succeeded in effecting great improvements. At first, moulds of the *single* columns were taken, and these, arranged in a forme of four pages, were secured on to the cylinder in the way I have described; but, by means of a roller-press, it was found possible to form a *papier-maché matrix of the whole large page*, and, of course, the mould being once made, the metal plate was easily cast. Now came another step in the forward direction. The 'casting-box' was *curved*, so as to fit the centre cylinder of the machine; the papier-maché mould was pressed in, and made to fit to the shape of the curved casting-box; so that when the melted metal had been poured in, and *set*, there was the stereotype plate of type, the size of the entire page, *ready curved* to suit the cylinder, and in about twenty minutes from the commencement of the process, could be easily and quickly secured on to the cylinder. Was not *that* a great step gained from the laborious method of building up the movable type in its chase and furniture upon the surface of the cylinder?"

"Well done, well done," exclaimed the Books.

"And did these curved stereotype plates succeed?" asked the Great Folio, when quiet was restored.

"Entirely so; by 1860, most, if not all, the printing at the *Times* office was done by these plates," replied the New Book. "Besides the saving of time and labour, they are found to save the type itself so much that a 'fount' will last nearly ten times as long as it used to do."

"Well, surely, your Mr. Walter and his companions were satisfied then?" said the Senior Defoe.

"But they were not; there is no staying the tide of progress, no quieting the busy brains, no satisfying the restless desires of men—some men, at least," replied the New Book.

"No, indeed; why Phæthon and Prometheus were tame and dull in their ambitions compared to your inventors of the present day," said the Virgil.

"What more did these most ambitious men desire and contrive to effect?" asked the Elzevir.

"Well, they were audacious enough to think that they should like to have a machine that could print from a *reel of paper*, instead of being fed by *separate sheets;* a machine that should *print both sides* of this roll paper;—worse still, that this one machine should unroll the paper; *damp* the paper; ink the formes; *print* the paper on both sides; cut the printed paper into sheets; take note how many sheets were cut; and turn the perfected sheets on to the desks of the 'takers-off.' And all this, these audacious men desired should be accomplished in one half the time, and with one half the labour, required by the then existing methods. What do you think of such ambitions?" said the New Book.

"Why, that the men were dreamers, and dreamed dreams far wilder than ever entered into the waking or sleeping hours of ancient or modern poet. That is my candid opinion, as you ask for it," said the Virgil.

"But do you really think such a machine can or ever will be contrived; one that can do all the things you have mentioned?" inquired the Great Folio.

"It has been done; these things are being performed every day; the dream has turned into *fact*—steady every-day *fact*—fact more wonderful far than dreams!" exclaimed the New Book, with considerable excitement. A general rustling and pressing forward showed that the members of the book society were also excited, and anxious for the New Book to continue.

"Such things, of course, cannot be brought about in a day," resumed the New Book. "The world sees the results of the toil, enjoys the fruits of the labour, feels them to be wonderful and pleasant, and bestows a portion of its favours on the successful labourers; but thinks little, and knows less, of the time, and the thought, and the care bestowed,—of the numberless experiments that have to be made,—the difficulties, the failures, the disappointments that attend and surround every single step of the way, from the first dim dawning of the thought, to the crowning perfected success of any great invention. It was so in this case. Each individual detail of the whole large scheme had to be thought about, and talked over, and planned, and executed, and tried over and over again, and in varieties of ways, as if it, and it alone, had been the one thing about the conquering of which they were concerned.

" For instance, the curved stereotype plates had to be yet more curved; each one had to be bent into a half-circle, or nearly so. Then, in a great complicated affair like this one, the alteration of one part would require the complete re-adjustment of another, and that again of another part. You yourselves can easily imagine how a kind of inking-roller, for instance, that answered admirably for one kind of machine, might not at all suit another sort of machine. A different form of inking-roller and inking apparatus must therefore be devised; and when devised, it must be tried over and over again. And so on with every detail that can be thought of as belonging to a large machine, intended to perform so many different operations. But Mr. John Walter, and Mr. J. C. Macdonald, the manager, and Mr. Calverley, the head engineer, worked on and on, ' unhasting and unresting,' till, by 1869, not only had the difficulties been overcome, not only had the first machine gone through all its preparatory trials, but four machines had been made, and were at daily work in the printing-office of the *Times*, and answering to the full all the ambitious desires of these daring projectors. Shortly after, two other machines were manufactured on Mr. Walter's premises, for the *Scotsman* paper. These two newest and latest machines not only exhibited all the principles of the others, but combined some special improvements of their own. Every difference in the requirements necessitates, as I said before, some alterations in the machinery. For instance, the paper on which the *Times* is printed is thick and costly; that on which the *Scotsman* is printed is thin and cheap; and, as you will all admit, it may be possible to do certain things with a paper of strength and substance, which it might not be possible to manage with a paper thin and weak in texture. Then the machinery that would cut one *uniform size* of paper, would not be adapted for cutting different sizes.

" But there is no daunting men of real genius, high courage, and determined purpose. Ere long the two new machines were adapted to the new conditions, and answered to the additional requirements; that is to say, *thin* paper was managed with the same results as the *thick*, and the cutting part of the machinery was made to cut *different* sizes of sheets, as well as one uniform size.

" The ' WALTER PRESS ' was a success ! "

A tumult of applause succeeded and lasted for some minutes. When it had subsided, the Great Folio begged for a short description of the machine itself, if the New Book could so far oblige them.

" I will do my best with the greatest pleasure," replied the New Book; "and I think you will be able to form some idea of the method and plan of proceeding. Please to try and imagine a long unbroken length of paper, made by the paper-making machine I have before described to you. This web of paper leaves the paper-machine in the form of a tightly-rolled reel, which weighs six hundredweight, and would, if unrolled, be found to be *four miles* in length. Arranged in a frame are four large cylinders, one above another. On the topmost of the four is placed the stereotype plate cast from the four pages of type which make the *inner forme*, and on the bottom cylinder the stereotype plate cast from the *outer forme* of type is put. The inking-rollers are arranged to the right and the left of the two printing cylinders, while the ink is pumped up from a reservoir in the floor.

"The reel of paper is placed at one end of the machine. The paper is guided, first of all, into a series of small cylinders where it gets *damped*. From the damping cylinders it is brought between the *first* and *second* of the large printing cylinders, and gets *printed on one side;* passes backwards between the *second* and *third* cylinders; then takes a forward direction, and goes between the *third* and *fourth* cylinders, and receives an impression on the second side from the type which is on the *fourth* cylinder.

" From these large cylinders the paper passes to other cylinders, where it gets cut into sheets of the required size, an index at the same moment registering the number of sheets cut.

"The sheets are then guided by tapes and drawn up an inclined plane, made to descend perpendicularly, until they reach a certain point in their course, when they are cast alternately backwards and forwards on to two boards, against which are sitting two boys, who lay hold of them and take them off. These two 'takers-off,' and a man to start the machine and look after the paper, are all the 'hands' which this wonderful machine requires in accomplishing its daily work.

"That work is, to damp the paper, ink the formes, *print on both sides,* and cut up into sheets a reel of paper four miles long *in less than twenty-five minutes,* turning out the *perfected sheets* at the rate of 12,000 an hour. The paper travels through the machine at the rate of 1,000 feet a minute ; and as it takes little more than a minute to put a fresh roll in the place of the one finished, the printing can go on and on with scarcely any intermission. In fact, thirty-six miles of paper are printed every morning at the *Scotsman* office by two of these Walter presses in *two hours,* or little more time than an ordinary train takes to go from Edinburgh to Glasgow. This and other facts were mentioned in an interesting article written last year on this press, first in the *Scotsman* newspaper, and then in the *Times ;* an article which was read with much delight in our society ; for I assure you we keep ourselves well up in the affairs of the day, especially those relating to the art to which we owe our existence as *Printed Books.* Said I not truly when I said that the Walter press was a brilliant success ? "

A general chorus of unqualified assent was heard from all parts of the room. After a short pause, the Great Folio remarked that listening to the wonderful accounts of the various improvements in the art of printing, and comparing the present methods with those which he could himself remember, made him feel how long a time he had been in the world—the backward steps seemed so many ; the beginnings of the art so far away in the distance.

"Yes," said the New Book, "if you put the old 'Screw' press, or the 'Improved' press of William Jansen Blaew, at one end of the hill, and this 'Walter' press at the other, the distance between the two seems to be considerable."

ı 2

" And so it does between the metal types cut by the hand of Gutenberg and these stereotype plates of four pages of type," said the Elzevir.

" And from the old dab, dab of the stuffed balls to the regular, even, gentle motion of the inking-rollers of which we have been told," said the Esop.

" Or, if you want another set of sign-posts, take the small yellow hand-made sheet of paper that we can, some of us, remember, and this long roll of four miles of machine-woven paper," said the Great Folio. " Truly, it is like looking down a steep precipice to look backwards down the years; and the things standing at the foot look very small, much smaller than they once appeared."

" Yes; but, venerable sir, you must remember that from the one to the other point of comparison, say from the Jansen Blaew press to the Walter press, there lies no unspanned gulf, no untravelled road; the distance may be great, the rock may be steep, but there are paths along the road, there are steps hewn in the rock—steps many and gradual from base to summit, hewn out by the labour, and thought, and patience, and courage of successive generations of men. On some few of the steps you will find the names of the workers carven upon them; but on the greater number far there is *no name*, nothing to tell of those who toiled to make them, and in toiling died. And yet had one of the many steps been missing, the Walter press had surely never stood on the proud eminence it occupies to-day."

" It would be a pleasant work to go over one by one the steps leading up to the result you have described; but our time would fail us," said the Great Folio.

" Yes, indeed it would," replied the New Book, " you should hear one of our modern philosophers talk of the multitude of small facts that go to make up one such great fact as a finished invention like the press we have been describing. You would feel we could never tell the twentieth part. It is so in all departments of science and art. Each successive improvement is the *result* of that which has gone before, the *cause* of that which comes after. And it is cheering to feel that all honest work, of head or hand, of heart or mind, no matter how small it may appear, however hidden it may remain, must, and does of necessity, help forward the world's progress and improvement."

"Certainly, the world seems to have become more and more exacting in the matter of newspapers. It is difficult to see where and when the demands will cease," remarked the Great Folio; after a slight pause, "I can recall the time when the *first* English newspaper made its appearance. It was on the 23rd of May, 1622, in the reign of King James I. It was thought a good deal of in those days, I dare say, though I must admit it was a rather poor affair. But, as I think I remarked before, there were a good number of weekly papers in circulation during the time of the civil wars. In fact, each of the rival armies carried about with it a printer."

"It is evident," said the New Book, "that the race of men called 'Our Special Correspondents' had not then made its appearance, or it would not have been needful to carry a printer and, I presume, all the printing apparatus about with the army baggage.

"You would be surprised if you knew the number of these 'specials' belonging to each of our leading papers of the present day; and amused at the remarkably strong family likeness between them, especially between those attached to the same paper. But I interrupt your account of the rise of the newspaper press."

"The fathers of the 'newspaper press' (as you phrase it) are, I think it will be generally allowed, Marchmont Needham, the Parliamentarian, and Sir John Birkenhead, the Royalist. Both rather violent and unscrupulous men. Anthony Wood, the antiquarian and historian, living at that time, does not speak particularly well of either of them; but, then, the clever antiquarian might be prejudiced. Marchmont Needham, it must be admitted, changed his politics to suit 'the times;' and as 'the times' changed rapidly and considerably in those days, Needham cannot be called a steadfast man. Then there was Roger L'Estrange, a clever man, who had rather an eventful life. He went with King Charles I. to Scotland, in 1639; was imprisoned as a spy in 1644, spent four years in prison, managed to escape and get abroad, returned in 1658, and got his living as an author, protected by the Act of indemnity passed by Cromwell. In 1663, he brought out, for the satisfaction and improvement of the people, the first number of his *Intelligencer*," continued the Great Folio.

"It did not continue long, I fancy?" said the Law Book.

"No; Sir Roger gave it up when the *London Gazette* appeared on the 1st of January, 1665."

"Was not that the year of the dreadful plague in London?" asked the Spenser.

"True; and the gazette was first called the *Oxford Gazette,* because, you know, the court had fled to Oxford. Sir Roger L'Estrange brought out, in 1679, another paper called the *Observator.*

"The number of papers rapidly increased," continued the Great Folio; "and before the year 1688 there were as many as seventy."

"Were any of these *daily* papers?" asked the New Book.

"No. The first daily morning paper was started in 1709, and was called the *Daily Courant,*" replied the Great Folio. "I believe the idea of having a sheet devoted to 'news,' and the word 'gazette,' as applied to such sheet, originated with the Venetians. They were at war with the Turks during the middle of the 16th century, and, of course, people were anxious for news of the war. The Government, in order to supply the desired information, published a paper *once a month,* and this paper was read aloud in the public places to any one who liked to pay the small coin called a 'gazetta' for the pleasure."

"Once a month! and a war going on!" exclaimed the New Book. "Well, certainly, people were more easily contented in those days than in the present."

"It is said, but I do not know with what certainty, that newspapers in my country owe their rise to the wisdom of a celebrated physician," said the French MS. "This doctor, whatever might be his skill in other ways, was very clever in collecting news, and he found that the hearing of news agreed with his patients. At any rate, it agreed with his purse, for people sent to him for his *news* whether or not they needed or cared for his medicine. So it struck him that he would give them a few regularly printed sheets of news every week, and obtained a privilege to do so in 1632."

"Clever man that," remarked the Esop; "evidently he understood human nature; at least as to its desire for news-feeding; and the propensity cannot be said to be on the decline. But you must excuse me if I remind the present company that the ancient Nuremberg claims the honour of giving to the world the first sheet of news-paper. It stands, I believe, on good authority, that a paper called the *Gazette* was published in that city in 1457. A very few years, you see, after Peter Schœffer had made his matrices, cast his first metal types, and obtained his Christina. "

"I ought to have mentioned," resumed the New Book, "that there are two other machines which, like the 'Walter,' not only print on both sides, but also rival the speed of the 'Hoe' machine, with less cost of manual labour. One of these is an American patent (the 'Bullock'), and the other a French patent (the 'Marinoni'). In 1868, M. Marinoni invented a machine that could perfect 10,000 full-sized sheets in an hour. Very soon afterwards, the proprietors of the *Echo* newspaper employed this kind of machine, and now for some time three, if not more, of them have been constantly at work in the office of the *Echo*, each turning out 20,000 copies per hour. But even with this rate of production, I assure you it is difficult to keep the supply equal to the demand."

"Pray, what are the principal features and advantages of this machine?" inquired the Great Folio.

"M. Marinoni's machine is, though strong, yet simple and light in construction, and not so costly as some others," replied the New Book. "It consists of six horizontal cylinders placed side by side, two cylinders for inking, two for the stereotype plates, and two for impressing. There are six 'layers-on,' who feed the machine, and the sheets, guided by tapes, pass on to the cylinders one after another, with the space of an inch between them. The 'taking-off' the printed sheets is managed by a very clever contrivance called the 'divider.' After a sheet is *perfected*, the set of tapes which have guided it pass over a set of small iron rollers in another direction, and release the sheet. The free sheets are then taken hold of by another set of tapes passing over other small rollers, and by them separated and guided in four different directions to four mechanical arms, called 'flyers,' which receive them and place them smoothly on four boards placed ready for them. Thus, without any confusion, the machine is cleared from the perfected sheets."

CHAPTER IX.

THE BINDING-SHOP.

"But to go back to my own personal history," resumed the New Book, after a silence. "When my sheets had been for a sufficient time in the hydraulic-press, where, if you remember, we left them, they were 'gathered;' that is to say, they were carefully arranged, according to the 'signatures,' in the proper order for 'folding,' and were then conveyed to the binders. The first thing done to them was to 'fold' them. This department of work, and many others connected with bookbinding, is under the care of women. We have 107 people at our place employed in bookbinding, and most of these, I am very glad to say, are women. Formerly, the 'gathered' sheets were placed on a board, and a woman used to fold them one after another by the aid of a thin paper-knife made of bone, and termed a 'folder,' and if a very quick worker she could get through perhaps 500 sheets an hour. But the folding is now done by means of machinery, which secures greater precision, and turns off a greater number. A woman can fold by the machine 1,200 or more sheets an hour, and this is a consideration, of course, since the introduction of the new Factories Act into bookbinding and printing offices; as this Act very wisely limits the labours of women and young persons to within certain hours. Now, when my sheets were folded, and laid one upon the other in a pile, I began to feel that I was coming out of the rudimentary and fragmentary state of my existence; that my individuality was beginning to assume a definite shape and form; and as I looked upon the several piles of similar sheets, I felt, with great complacency, what a large book I should certainly make. But not for long was I allowed to remain in this inflated state of mind with regard to my probable size as a book. My sheets were taken and placed once more in an hydraulic-press. They were next put between tinned iron

BOOK AND MAGAZINE FOLDING-MACHINE.

plates, and passed between two iron rollers, which glazed and compressed them very much."

"I can remember that we were beaten with a hammer on a stone," remarked the Senior Defoe; "but I suppose the purpose was the same."

"Yes; but this 'rolling-machine' compresses the sheets so very much more

ROLLING-MACHINE.

than the old 'hammering' did, it therefore makes a book much smaller and thinner than it would otherwise be; an advantage to the owner who wishes to have as many as he can on his shelves; but the result, on my mind, was to make me 'feel small,'" said the New Book. "We were then all 'collated'—that is, examined to see that the signatures ran properly. The plates were added, and the waste leaves at the beginning and end. My sheets were next taken to the 'saw-bench,' and by means of some small circular saws, arranged at certain regular distances, some grooves or slits were sharply cut in each sheet, through which the thread was to pass when the sheets were sewn together. I have six of these little grooves, but some of you, being larger, will have more."

SAW-BENCH.

"I have more, naturally," said the Great Folio; "and my holes were made by a man who first fixed me tight, and then took a saw and cut with it the requisite holes."

"From the saw-bench, my sheets were taken and laid, title uppermost, upon the 'sewing-table.' On this table was a frame, composed of a bottom board, two long upright screws, and a cross horizontal bar. Fastened to this bar and the bottom board were some tightly stretched tapes or cords. Sitting sideways by this frame was a woman. She took up my first sheet with the signature A, which you know contains my title, table of contents, &c., and placed it with the back to these 'bands,' so that a band came against the four middle grooves which the saw had made, leaving a hole at the top and bottom of the sheet without any band. The woman then placed her left hand inside the sheet, with her right she passed her needle, threaded with strong string, through the top hole which is made for the 'kettle' or catch-stitch, as it is called, leaving a piece of string. She returned the needle with her left hand through the first groove, then back again through the *same groove*, making the string go round the cord or band, pulled the string tight, and went on to the next groove, and so on, until she came to the last groove, for the bottom 'kettle' or catch-stitch,

SEWING SHEETS TOGETHER.

where she left a piece of string to be fastened afterwards. She then took another sheet and did as before, proceeding, however, from the bottom to the top. When she reached the top 'kettle-stitch,' she tied her thread to the bit of string left from the first sheet. After this she took two sheets at a time and sewed, or passed the needle through the grooves first of one of the sheets and then of the other. That sort of sewing I heard described as 'up and down' work. In some books the grooves are not sawn, but the sewer, taking each sheet singly, makes the necessary holes with her needle. Of course, that way of sewing requires more time and care, but books so sewn open more freely than those which are stitched in the ordinary way.

"When several books had been placed on the frame, and thus sewn, the tapes were cut, but a piece of each tape was left to each one of the books, in order afterwards to be fastened down to the boards. The sewing done, a layer of glue was passed over the back, and then a piece of coarse thin canvas, the exact length, but wider than the back, was pasted down, and the sewing made secure.

"And now, indeed, I felt that I was at last a *Book*, an individual Book, no more a mere number of loose disjointed *sheets*, but something compact, sewn, fastened together; and something, besides, which possessed a *Title !*"

" But you had no outer covering to you," said the French MS., " you were behind many a so-called *unbound* MS."

"True, I was far from being ' finished,' I possessed no external covering, no gaudy dress—I was not yet bound; but still I had the delightful conviction that I had a place in the world as a distinct individual. Already, I began to speculate as to where my future home would be, what kind of companions I should have, and what the scenes and pleasures through which I might pass. But I was yet to undergo a great deal of sharp usage before I was considered ready to be introduced to the world. First of all I was laid between two boards, and my edges made tidy and straight by a very sharp knife, but not cut quite through. When this was done, my back had to be shaped. I was tightly fastened in a machine, by means of which my back, which before had been quite flat, was formed into the proper curve.

" *Round* backs are, as you know, considered the correct thing in a well-shaped book, however they may be esteemed in other connections. My back was depressed at the sides and raised in the middle. The indentations or grooves made in the sides formed a place in which the cover-boards could be laid. It is astonishing how quickly and how easily the ' rounding ' and backing are done by the machines."

" In my days this ' rounding ' and ' forwarding ' were done by the workman's *blows*," said the Senior Defoe. " I can remember being tapped with a hammer first on one side and then on another, and my back drawn first this way and then the other.   Afterwards, if I remember, I was screwed tightly between boards in a

"ROUNDING" OR "BACKING" PRESS.

sort of screw-press, and a man gently hammered me, and, I suppose, produced those same grooves in the sides for my boards, which, in your case, were made by the machines you mention."

"The effect produced is much the same, doubtless," said the New Book; "but the ease, precision, and rapidity with which it is effected are so much greater with the one method than with the other and older ones. After the rounding of my back was accomplished, I was inclosed in a thin case, and placed with a number of companions between wooden boards with our backs projecting, and put into a 'standing-press,' the upper part of which press was screwed down upon us

OLD METHOD OF ROUNDING BOOKS.

with great force. There we were left for some hours, that we might become sufficiently *compressed*. I can only speak for myself, but I know I felt as considerably depressed in mind as I was compressed in dimensions."

"Well, you *printed* books have certainly a great deal to pass through before you arrive at perfection. We MSS. are longer in hand, but our treatment is much less severe. I think, on the whole, if you will excuse my making the remark, I much prefer to be a MS. and not a printed book, and perhaps I shall last as long as any of you."

"I think that is extremely probable in the case of your ladyship," replied the New Book, politely, "though it would not be so in the case of every MS. Now I will tell you about the way in which my outer dress is made, for I have often heard it described."

"Oh, pray, let us hear all about our fine coat," said some Book in the background, who evidently considered the outside to be the most important part of a book, and who was envious of the New Book's superiority in this respect.

"My outer coat is of cloth, woven cloth," continued the New Book. "I will not take you to Manchester, where this particular kind of cloth is made, and show you the loom and the processes of weaving, lest we should never get back again to London and our subject. I will only say that this cloth is prepared in Manchester, and sent up to London, where it is dyed different colours, and glazed, and embossed, or 'grained,' as it is called, and then sent to the binders in rolls of forty-six yards, thirty-six inches wide.

"When it gets to the binders it is cut up into the proper sizes for the books. An extra piece must be always allowed for the turning down, as you will presently see. The inside of my coat is formed of stout 'mill-board.' These mill-boards are sent to the binders in sheets of different sizes, and can be cut by means of a machine with wonderful precision and rapidity to the size required for the books."

"I possess solid wood for my covering," said the Quarto, displaying the interior of his coat, from which all the lining had disappeared.

"So I perceive," replied the New Book, "and that makes you weighty, not to say ponderous. Your outside covering may be said to be homogeneous with your internal character."

"I think I do not quite discern your meaning," said the Quarto; "that word you used, perhaps I did not catch it."

"Oh, it only means, as you know, of like nature," replied the New Book. "I meant no offence."

"I see, yes, exactly ; I always wish to be consistent," rejoined the Quarto, who evidently took the remark as a compliment.

" In making 'cloth cases,'" resumed the New Book, " there are two men employed. One man takes the cloth cover and puts a layer of glue inside. He

STEAM BLOCKING-PRESS.

then lays the cut pieces of mill-board in their proper position in the inside of the cover, leaving, of course, the space between the boards equal to the thickness of

J

the back of the book, turns the case over, and rubs it with a cloth rubber.   That is all he has to do ; so he tosses the case to the other man, who places a piece of canvas along the inside of the back, folds the projecting edges of the cloth upon the boards, and smoothes them down with the edge of a flat piece of steel.   This piece of steel has a blunt point at each end, and the man draws that down along the boundary lines of the back and sides, and thus makes the little ridge to be seen there.   You perceive that there are a good many things to be done, yet these two men can turn off one hundred covers thus far prepared in an hour."

"But you have said nothing about the ornamentation of your cover," said the French MS. ; "I am curious to hear how that is made."

"I am just coming to that part of the work," replied the New Book. "Cloth covers are embossed *after* the boards are put in, leather covers *before;* but as we are talking about *cloth covers,* I will tell you first of all how they are embossed and gilded.   The 'blocking-presses' for embossing (especially those used for embossing leather) are formidable-looking things, consisting of a strong solid iron frame.   The pattern is first cut in a thick plate of brass or steel, and the 'block' fixed in the upper part of the press, and heated by gas.   The cloth cover to be ornamented is carefully arranged on the lower part of the press, and then the upper bed of the press is brought down with great force upon the lower, and the cloth receives the impression.

"In embossing leather, there is not only the 'metal die,' but there is what is called the 'counter die.'   The metal die is fixed upon the *lower* bed of the press, and heated by gas.   Several sheets of mill-board, glued together, are fastened to the upper bed—the upper bed is brought down with great force upon the lower bed, and the mill-board takes the impression of the metal die, forming, of course, the reverse, or *counter* impression.   This 'counter die,' after being trimmed and shaped a little, is fastened to the upper bed of the press, the leather arranged, and when the upper bed is brought down strongly upon the lower one, the leather is forced into and against the metal die, and the pattern becomes embossed.

"After the cloth has been embossed, the gilt letters and ornaments are impressed.   The parts of the case where the gilt is to come are first of all covered over with a thin layer of white of egg, and then with a film of gold leaf, which clings to the 'glaire,' as it is called. The covers are next taken to the 'gold-blocking press.' I ought to have told you that when ornaments are simply

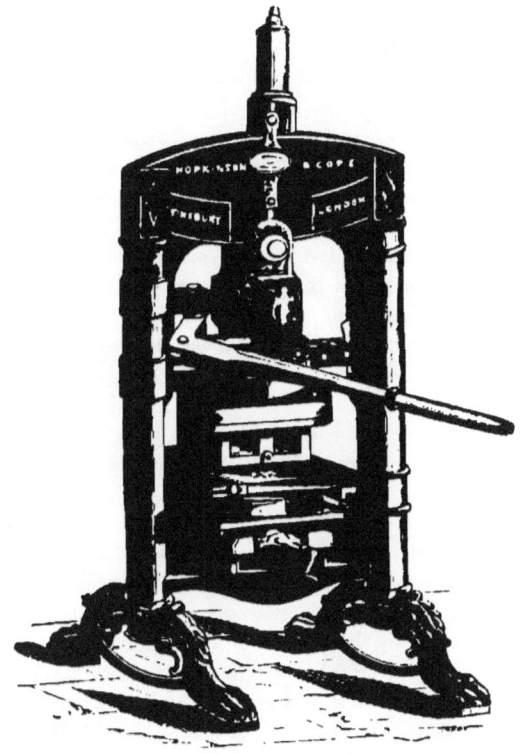

HAND BLOCKING-PRESS.

produced by *pressure*, the operation is called 'blind blocking;' when done by hand and separate tools, 'blind tooling.' So with the gilt letters and gilt ornaments, if

L 2

they are done by pressure, the case is said to be 'gold blocked;' if by hand, 'gold tooled.' Cloth cases are generally 'blind blocked' and 'gold blocked.' The ornaments are first cut out of a solid piece of brass, the letters are either set up in movable type or cut out of one piece of brass. Both ornaments and letters are arranged upon a plate or block in the upper bed of the 'gold-blocking press.' This plate is kept heated by jets of gas which are arranged in the upper bed. The cover which is to be impressed is carefully laid on a bed in the lower part. A man, who sits in front of the press, moves a handle round, which brings the heated plate down with a gentle even pressure upon the cloth beneath, and the ornaments and letters are fixed upon the cover. When the cover comes out of the press, a boy wipes off all the superfluous gold with a piece of thick rag or soft india-rubber, specially prepared; and though you would hardly believe it, this rag or india-rubber becomes in two or three months so valuable that it will be sold to a gold-refiner for as much as twenty or thirty shillings."

"Why, whatever can he do with it?" asked the Senior Defoe.

"He burns it in a covered crucible, and so recovers the precious metal," replied his junior relative.

"Well, that is making the most of things truly," said the Esop.

"And now, my cover being fully made and duly ornamented," continued the New Book, "the happy moment arrived in which it was to be fitted upon me, and made a part of me, so to speak. You may remember, perhaps, that I noticed to you, that when the piece of canvas was glued upon my back, after the sewing of the sheets, the canvas was wider than my back. This strip of projecting canvas on each side was now glued on to each of the boards of my cover, and by this means my dress was securely fastened on to me; and a piece of coloured lining-paper being glued in the inside, every thing was made tidy and complete. I was sent back to the 'standing-press' for a few hours; and when released from that, then, indeed, I felt and knew that I was a Book, a bound and ornamented Book. The pride of that moment I shall not soon forget. No young lady just leaving school ever rejoiced more heartily at having, as she considered, 'finished her education,' than did I as I emerged from the hands of the binder, a *finished book*. And I had a great deal more reason to consider myself *finished* than any young lady has who is just fresh from school, for, poor thing, her education, strictly speaking, is only then about to commence. But I am sure you will all be able to recall your own feelings on a like occasion, and can understand and sympathise with mine."

"Very true; I have no doubt we all felt more or less elated at that time," said the Quarto. "But you are bound in *cloth*, and what you have described to us is the manner of binding in cloth. But what about books that, like myself, are bound in *leather?* I am 'embossed,' as you call it, and somewhat elaborately, and my coat has worn extremely well. Perhaps anything so solid and lasting as leather is not considered desirable or necessary for the books of the present day."

"I beg your pardon," replied the New Book, slightly ruffled. "But if in these days we try by cheap books to bring knowledge and wisdom, the gathered fruit of the past, and the living flower of the present, within the reach of the *many* as well as of the few, and present them also in forms and colours that are tasteful though not costly, yet, I assure you, we delight to produce books that are very marvels in elegance and beauty of design, and in skill and delicacy of workmanship. I have heard of a book bound in morocco by Hayday, our celebrated English binder, in which more than 57,000 tool impressions were required. Pretty well that, I think, for a manufacturing age, which is said not to care for elaborate workmanship.

"If a book bears upon it the words, in golden letters, 'Bound by Hayday,' it is enough to make that book valuable. And in the Exhibition of 1862, Mr. Francis Bedford took, according to the 'jurors' report,' the first rank among both English and foreign binders; though I must in honesty mention that one at least of the most celebrated French houses was unrepresented at the competition, which might perhaps have carried the palm. At the same Exhibition, there were some splendid bindings shown by Messrs. Engelmann and Graf, of Paris. In one book—a devotional one, called 'Hours of the Middle Ages,' a thin octavo—the elaboration was so great, that one volume was priced at seven pounds. And there was also an illustrated edition of Dante, with a photograph of the poet, exhibited by Decker from Berlin, the price of which for a copy upon vellum was £200; and a copy upon fine paper £2 9s. So you see we do know how to value things that are beautiful in design and elaborate in workmanship. But I was going to add a few words on the more finished and elaborate class of binding.

"The differences in the processes are not so very great. When a book is to be bound in leather, the boards are added after the operations of sewing and gluing and rounding the back are completed. The boards have been first cut to

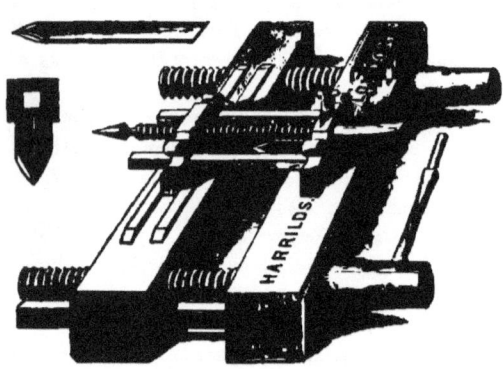

the proper size, and then two holes are made in each board opposite each band, and the pieces of the bands which the sewer left are put through the holes and fastened down with glue."

"That is exactly the way in which my boards were fastened," said the Quarto. "The inner lining of my coat being so completely worn away, you can see the holes and the cords."

"Very easily indeed,"

"PLOUGH" CUTTING-MACHINE.

said the New Book, "and I perceive that you have had four 'bands' sewn into you; therefore you have eight holes in each of your boards. After the boards are properly secured, the edges of the book are cut right through, so that no after cutting with the paper knife is required. Many of you in this room were, I suspect, placed in what is called the 'bookbinder's press,' and had your edges cut through with what is known as the 'bookbinder's plough.' The press, if you remember, consists of two strong pieces of wood connected by two wooden screws. The plough is made of two upright pieces of wood fastened together by a screw. To one of the upright pieces of wood, called 'cheeks,' is fixed a knife with a double-edged, pointed blade. The book whose edges were to be

"GUILLOTINE" CUTTING-MACHINE.

'ploughed' was screwed up tightly in the press. One of the sides of the plough was placed in a groove on one side of the press, and the knife was moved backwards and forwards against the book; the man, by twisting the handle of the screw of the plough, pushed the knife forward till the cutting was done. But this cutting of the edges is now performed by a very different machine to the old plough. The book is laid on an iron table, made fast, and a long sharp knife made to descend on the edges, which does the work in an instant. This machine goes by the name of the 'Guillotine' cutting-machine—a name of ill omen, I am aware."

"The edges of printed books are, I notice, often gilt and coloured various colours," said the French MS. "How is that managed?"

"Where edges are gilt, as you see mine are," replied the New Book, "a thin layer of white of egg is laid over them, and then gold leaf applied, which clings to them. The edges are well rubbed with a tool called the 'burnisher,' made of agate, which is an exceedingly hard stone. This fixes the gold, and polishes it at the same time. With some books the white edges have a little colour sprinkled over them, which helps to keep them clean. Some coloured chalks, umber, Venetian red, ochre, and others, are mixed with size and water. The book to be sprinkled is firmly fixed between two boards, a man holds a piece of wood a few feet above the book, dips a brush into the mixture, and dashes the hairs of the brush upon the piece of wood. As you may suppose, a shower of minute drops of colour falls upon the edges, which are then polished with the agate burnisher."

"Is that the way in which the odd nondescript coloured streaks or patterns on some edges are produced?" inquired the English MS.

"No; 'marbled edges' are done in another way," replied the New Book. "A number of coloured substances are ground to a fine powder in spirits of wine, and the powder is thrown upon the surface of a trough, two inches deep, of gum and water. By means of a quill and a comb the coloured powders are made to arrange themselves in various forms; the edges of the book are just lightly dipped into the trough, when the colours settle themselves on to the edges, and a little cold water applied afterwards fixes them and brightens the tints, which are afterwards polished with a burnisher.

"You will notice in many books that there is a little 'head-band.' Our learned friend the Quarto has one, though I see that the once plaited strings are now hanging loosely. These head-bands are put on while a book is still in boards. The book is made fast by one corner in the screw-press. A man takes a thin slip of mill-board, fastens it with a needle and thread through the top part of the back of the book, twists or plaits a coloured silk or thread over the strip, and fastens it down with the needle. When a band is made in that way it is said to be ' worked.' But there is a way of doing it for common bindings, when it is said to be ' stuck on.' A piece of cord is rolled in a bit of coloured linen, and ' stuck on ' with glue. Sometimes, also, there are raised bands down the back, across the part where a book has been stitched. Our friend the Quarto has four such raised projections, and they are made by gluing strips of mill-board, cord, or leather across."

"Now, I suppose, the book is ready to be covered when the ' head-band' has been completed?" said the English MS.

" Yes. The leather, whether it is morocco, or russia, or calf, the skin must be chosen free from blemishes. We must not stop to talk of the way in which leather is manufactured; but I may just remind you that the substance called leather is the inner or ' true skin ' of the animal, united—chemically united— with some other substance, generally tannin or tannic acid; by which union the fibrous animal membrane becomes possessed of peculiar properties. The leather being cut into the proper size for the book, and embossed, is laid on a board, and the edges pared with a sharp knife, to make them lie smoothly when turned over. The leather cover is first damped, paste is put over, and then the cover applied to the book, and by means of a few tools is easily adjusted. The workman takes care to smooth the edges, and raise the bands at the back. When that is done, he puts in the lining-papers; and after the books have been pressed for a short time, they are ready for the gold and other ornaments to be added. In all the best class of bindings, these ornaments are applied by hand, and not by the 'blocking-press,' and then the bindings are said to be ' blind tooled' and ' gold tooled.'

" The ' tools ' employed are not very many. The blind-tool ornaments are cut out in pieces of brass, and the brass fastened on to handles, and when heated the workman passes them over the cover. You often see a long line or 'roll ' running up the sides of a book, and that is produced in this way. A line is cut upon the edge of a circular bit of brass, the bit of brass is made to turn on a centre axis, and put into a long handle. The man rests the handle against his shoulder, and rolls the tool up the side of the book. The parts where the gold ornaments are to come are first covered with white of egg, and then with gold-leaf. The heated tool is pressed upon the part, and the gold-leaf remains fastened. All the tools are kept heated by a gas-stove."

"That will be less unwholesome than the charcoal brazier, which was used in my day," remarked the Mystery.

BOOKBINDER'S TOOLS AND GAS-STOVE.

"When the ornamenting and lettering are done, the cover is polished and finished by polishing irons of different shapes and sizes, and after that is pronounced to be 'finished.'"

"It seems to me that I can recall the time of my own bringing-up," said the Senior Defoe, "and almost the sensations I then experienced. Things —processes in bookbinding—do not strike me as being so very greatly altered since the days when I was young."

"Perhaps not as to the main features," replied the New Book; "but I suspect there is a marvellous difference in the speed at which work is turned off. In the present day, division of labour is so largely carried out, the hands employed are so numerous, and the mechanical contrivances for saving time and labour are so varied, that the amount of work accomplished in a short period of time would be incredible to the binders of past days.

" FINISHING."

"In the course of six hours a book can be 'gathered, folded, collated, sewn, glued, rounded, edges cut, mounted in covers, pressed, and finished.' The covers, I allow, must be prepared beforehand, but then 1,000 covers can be made ready in less than two days."

"I cannot see why your 'cheap' books require to be ornamented at all," said the Quarto. "It may be desirable for the advancement of learning, that

books should be produced cheaply; but the cost of ornamentation might surely
be spared. And then, again, why should money and time be spent in making
things elegant and beautiful that are both common and ephemeral?"

"As to that," said the Spenser, "the flowers fade quickly, yet what more
beautiful, more delicately made, than the blossom that lives perhaps but a
few hours. Nature is no niggard; she showers her beauties on the commonest
things as well as the uncommon. Listen to what my dear master, Mr. Edmund
Spenser says:

> 'Good is not good unless it be spend;
> God giveth good to none other end.'"

"A very true and noble sentiment of Mr. Spenser's," said the Great Folio;
"but still I am rather inclined to our friend the Quarto's opinion, and to think
it almost a pity that much care and trouble should be given to the outside,
when it is the inner part that can alone impart wisdom."

(The Folio was dressed, it must be remembered, in the very plainest of plain
bindings, not that that can be supposed to have had anything to do with his
opinion on the matter.)

"Well, I am, as you know, but young," said the New Book, "and naturally
like that which is pretty; but I must say that I think pretty things are *useful*
as well as *pleasant*. Surely, when a book presents to the eye forms that are
elegant and colours that are harmonious, the *outside* of that book does its part
as well as the *inside*, in diffusing correct ideas and spreading abroad the
knowledge of that which is good and true. And however simple and inexpensive
the ornamentation and general 'getting-up' of a book may be, there is no
reason that a 'cheap' book should not, in its degree, perform this office as well
as the most costly."

CHAPTER X.

HISTORY OF BOOKBINDING.

" I HOPE you *printed* books do not imagine for a moment that the art of binding was unknown to the world before the art of printing was discovered, because, I can assure you, you are mistaken if you do," remarked the French MS. " I know that MS. books were often bound in the old monasteries in strong boards of oak, and that not unfrequently these boards were richly ornamented with precious stones. Not that these ornaments were always visible at a first glance; but if you touched a secret spring, in what appeared to be solid wood, a little sort of cupboard opened out, and in that lay the concealed ornaments."

" That reminds me," said the Folio, " that, in the times of our civil wars, similar hollow covers of books were often used as places of concealment for money; but I am interrupting your ladyship, which is a mistake on my part, for I am sure you must have seen in your life many specimens of splendid bindings, and can have much to tell us on the subject."

" That is true. I have seen bindings rare and costly, gorgeous and beautiful, during my life, and most of all in my own dear France," replied the French MS. with enthusiasm. " Of course, it was not long before the oak boards were covered with leather; sometimes with velvet; sometimes, later on, with silk. MSS., and, I believe, even some of the very early printed books, were sometimes bound in rough, undressed skins; but quite as early as the beginning of the fifteenth century *vellum* began to be used as a binding. At first it was quite plain, and the edges made so as almost to meet in the centre."

" That would be a good way of preserving the edges of the book itself," said the Law Book, whose old parchment cover had to some extent done him this good service.

"Yes, doubtless, many a book owes in part its preservation to this custom," replied the French MS. "But in the next century vellum bindings began to be-stamped. The vellum was stretched out upon a board and then 'tooled' in arabesque patterns. The effect was very lovely. I have heard that morocco binding was introduced by the celebrated Abbé Grolier, as early as 1494. A wonderful collector of books was the Abbé, and all his books were bound in the most splendid and elegant manner. A man of great and high taste, and of most princely liberality as well, for he loved to *share* his treasures with others, and his choice books, with their superb bindings, bore upon them this inscription :—

‘ Joannis Grollier et amicorum.’ "

"Well, the good Abbé was certainly very different from most of the book collectors I have known ; they have generally been unwilling to allow any one to enjoy their treasures with them," said the Esop.

"Then there was James Augustus de Thou, the son of Christopher de Thou, the first President of the Parliament of France, who was a very great collector. It is said that he spent 20,000 crowns on the binding alone of his books. They were bound in red and olive morocco, and had the wreathed arms and Latinised name of their owner stamped in gold on their sides, and his monogram on their backs. These two men, De Thou and Grolier, used to have paper manufactured expressly for them when they desired anything extra fine and good. De Thou left an immense library, with orders that it should never be broken up."

"And where is it now ?" asked the English MS.

"Alas ! it was sold at a public sale, so I heard from a friend, shortly before the dreadful Revolution ; and who can say where the treasures are now ?" replied the French MS. "Morocco binding was in such request among the connoisseurs, that M. Colbert, one of the ministers of Louis XIV., made a treaty with the Emperor of Morocco for a certain number of real morocco skins to be sent yearly from Africa, and this morocco was to be employed in binding books for the royal library of Paris."

EXAMPLE OF GROLIER BINDING.

"Was there not some French statesman about this time who suffered rather severely for putting his motto upon his books?" inquired the Quarto.

"You mean, perhaps, Fouquet, minister in Louis XIV.'s time. His books were all inscribed with his arms, a squirrel, and the motto, "Whither shall I not ascend." This motto was looked upon as a sign of his great ambition, and the poor man fell under the king's displeasure, and his property was confiscated."

"That was paying dearly for a little vanity," said the Esop.

"Bookbinding in those days, at least in my country, was not a mere *trade*; it was a profession and an art practised by the learned and the wealthy. De Seuil, for instance, Abbé though he was, was a *bookbinder*, and so clever in the art that books bound by his hand are considered almost priceless."

"Yes, this famous Abbé De Seuil," said the Elzevir, "bound a book printed by our firm, which goes by the name of 'The Elzevir Cicero of 1642.' He bound it in old olive-coloured morocco, and lined it with red morocco, the edges gilt and marbled. This 'Elzevir Cicero of 1642' has a history of its own. It was in ten volumes, and once belonged to the library of Count Hoyau, ambassador from the King of Poland to your King Louis XIV. The count was a great collector of choice books, and his books were always decorated with his arms, two *fasces*, or parallel bands; and I have been told that whenever that mark can be found on the binding of a book, the value of that book is very greatly increased. The count's library was sold in 1738. It must have been a large one, for the sale lasted fifty-nine days. Of course, one cannot help feeling interested in the fate of such a book, coming from so celebrated a firm, if I may be pardoned for saying so, as the 'Elzevir Brothers;' and I overheard, accidentally, that this very same Cicero was sold in 1859 for a good sum, at the sale of M. Libri's books."

"It was a favoured book," remarked the Virgil; "author, printer, binder —all illustrious."

"Fifty-nine days was indeed a long time for a sale of books to last," said the Great Folio; "and I should think this must be one of the longest, if not the very longest, sale on record. But I know we had one in England that lasted forty-two days. It was called 'The Roxburghe sale,' and took place in the early part of this century."

EXAMPLE OF "GOLD TOOLING."

" Ah, that was indeed a time of excitement, and a time of great triumph
for books which belonged to our generation, and still more to those of the pre-

K

ceding one," said the Elzevir. " It would be quite difficult to make a modern Book—our young friend, for instance—understand the value attaching in the eyes of a real lover of old books to a genuine ' *Editio princeps,*' or to a book that has been bound by some celebrated hand ; or to one that possesses some old distinguishing trait, such as a ' Colophon.' "

" O, pray, explain the meaning of that," said the French MS.

" Before title-pages were used," replied the Elzevir, " the *last page* of a book contained the date and place of publication, printer's name, &c. ; and an end page thus inscribed is called a ' Colophon.' But I was going to say that in this great battle—this ' Waterloo among book-battles,' as I have heard it called by that odd, clever Dr. Frognal Dibdin—the excitement was tremendous, and the prices paid almost incredible. A book printed by Caxton, repaired by that Mrs. Weir who, you know, was clever at that kind of work (in fact, she was a regular doctress of old worn books), and bound by the great binder Roger Payne, fetched the sum of £360. That seems considerable ; but what will you say when I tell you that an ' *Editio princeps*' of Boccaccio, printed in Venice in 1474, was actually sold to the Marquis of Blandford for £2,260 ? "

" I suppose it was the fact of its being one of the *first edition* that made it so valuable in the eyes of the collectors," said the New Book ; " but it seems strange to me that it should be so ; for I know in these days that many people purposely wait until the first edition of a book is ' out,' because they think the next will be cheaper."

" Indeed ! Well, I have no sympathy with that kind of feeling," replied the Elzevir. " But in the case of this particular Venetian Boccaccio, you see it was so rare that the edition was not known to be in existence. Even the Paris library did not possess a copy. You consider us to be old, and we flatter our-selves that we are so ; yet none of us can boast of the distinguishing marks which belong to one of these valued *bona fide* ' *Editio princeps.*' None of us can show the two solid planks of oak, the undressed skin covering, the queer type, like the handwriting of the day, and the decorated capital letter of the book that issued from the very earliest presses of 400 years ago. No wonder all genuine lovers of old books are anxious to possess such a one."

" You mentioned just now a M. Libri," remarked the French MS. " *He* was indeed a great collector, and possessed a magnificent library, containing, among other treasures, books that once belonged to royal personages. There were several books of Mesdames, daughters of Louis XV., all splendidly bound in morocco, with the arms of France on each side. Each of these royal ladies had her own special favourite colour. All the books of Madame Adelaide's were bound in *red* morocco; those of Madame Sophie's in *citron ;* and those of Madame Victoire's in *green* or olive."

" I am afraid we English were rather behind your nation in the matter of splendid bindings," said the Great Folio ; " yet our King Henry VIII. had many superb volumes bound in oak boards, covered with velvet, and ornamented with gold bosses and other devices. But whether they were the work of native artists I cannot say. I have heard that most of the designs for ornamental bindings at that time were the work of the painter Holbein, who was a great friend of Sir Thomas More's, and was by him introduced to our King Henry. Gold tooling is said to have been first practised in England in this reign. In Queen Elizabeth's reign it was rather fashionable to *embroider* the covers of the better kinds of books. The Queen herself used to spend her spare time in embroidering covers for Bibles and devotional books with gold and silver thread and coloured silks. That we had also good plain, yet lasting binding, as well as these fancy kinds, you may see from our good friend the Quarto, whose thick, embossed leather coat has worn most remarkably well."

" Later down there seems to have been a great liking for dark calf bindings, ornamented with gilt," said the Quarto ; " and in the reign of George II. the ' Cambridge binding,' as it was called, came into fashion—sober, grey-tinted calf, with bands in which the interstices were filled with gold. The effect was certainly very good."

" Do you remember that clever bookbinder and most eccentric man, old Roger Payne?" said the Senior Defoe, addressing himself to the Great Folio.

" You mean the Roger Payne who had his workshop, so I heard, in Leicester Square, during the reign of George III., but who lived almost entirely in his

K 2

cellar, I suppose," replied the Great Folio. "He was a most wonderful hand at his trade, especially in the binding of old and rare books."

"Yes, for a book to have stamped upon it, 'Bound by Roger Payne,' is to ensure its good reception into the best circles, I am told," said the Senior Defoe.

"Certainly, he did his work well," said the Great Folio; "and he did it all himself, from the first to the last, making even his own tools. You may know his books by the beauty and excellence of the 'tooling,' the good taste displayed in their ornaments, and the capital manner in which their backs are 'forwarded.'"

"I wish it had been my good fortune to be 'bound by Roger Payne.' I suspect I should have been more valued than I am now," said the Senior Defoe, rather ruefully; "but I used to hear a great deal about him and his ways and his books. Pity it was that the man had such bad habits, for he might have been very rich. Earl Spenser, I know, patronised him very much, and he bound a copy of Æschylus for that nobleman in the most splendid style. He charged between £15 and £16 for the binding of that book; but, then, it must have been worth it, for, as he set forth in his bill (a bill which somehow got talked about among the books in the bookseller's where I once spent a little time), 'it was embordered with ermine, expressive of the high rank of the noble patroness of the designs' (the earl's wife, I believe); and, as he further states—partly, I suppose, in apology for the sum he charged—'It takes a great deal of time making out the measurements, preparing the tools, and making out new patterns.' Truly, an eccentric man was Roger Payne; but there have been few such binders before or since."

"May I ask, while I think of it," said the New Book, "whether any of you in this room knew a Mr. Riebau, who had a book-shop in Blandford Street?"

No one seemed able to answer the question.

"For what were his books most remarkable, or was he himself a great lover and collector of them?" asked the Great Folio, who evidently considered, as was perhaps natural, that the man was of little consequence compared to his books.

"I know nothing at all remarkable about the man, nor about his books," replied the New Book; "all I know is, that Mr. George Riebau once had a young lad as an apprentice who afterwards became very celebrated."

" Ah, another Roger Payne, perhaps," remarked the Senior Defoe.

"O dear, no; nothing of the sort," replied the New Book, rather ruffled. " This young lad, though he did his duty by his master honestly and well, was not, like your Roger Payne, devoted to the mysteries of bookbinding, and delighting in the fingering and ornamenting of the *outside ;* it was the *inner* part of a book that attracted the young apprentice, thirsting for knowledge. One day, when he was engaged in the binding of an encyclopædia, an article in it upon electricity caught his attention, and from that time he determined to devote himself to the study of science. He read all that he could find on his master's shelves, from Mrs. Marcet's ' Conversations on Chemistry' upwards ; studied and made experiments, and in after years his name became known to the world as one of its greatest and grandest in the roll of searchers after, and lovers of, the truth in science, especially in the departments of magnetism and electricity. I do assure you, that there are few names pronounced with greater love and reverence than the name of MICHAEL FARADAY, once a 'prentice-lad to the trade of binding books."

This announcement did not appear to awaken the amount of enthusiasm the New Book expected.

" You are disappointed in us, my young friend," said the Esop, half kindly, half cynically ; " but you must remember that though we are eminently a *literary* society, yet that men and things merely scientific have not the same attraction for us as the things have which are more particularly connected with our own interests. It may be different with you who have mingled more in the present world, and heard talk of the things now going on in that world. And then, you see, we are somewhat like a certain fox of classical reputation—we are apt to look upon things which cannot or do not come within our reach as being unfit to be gathered, not worth the trouble."

" You are not alone in that peculiarity, I fancy," said the New Book, good-temperedly. " But speaking of great collectors of books, I dare say some of you may have known, or been in some way connected with, Mr. Richard Heber, who must have had an immense number of books, for I have heard that the catalogues consisted of five thick octavo volumes ; and that the sale of his books, in 1834, perhaps was the largest known."

"Yes, he was a friend of our late owner's, and the most industrious and determined collector of books that ever lived. He had three or four houses in London filled with books from garret to cellar—chairs, tables, passages, every part covered with *books*—books everywhere, nothing but books. Then he had libraries at Oxford, Paris, Brussels, Ghent, Antwerp, and other places. Well might the mere lists of them occupy some volumes," said the Folio.

"But then, you see, when a man dies, all these treasures get scattered abroad, and must many of them be lost," said the French MS. "That appears to me the worst of these large *private* libraries."

"That is true; but by being dispersed, they become known, and so serve their purpose better than when stowed away in a private or public library," replied the New Book.

"Ah, but numbers of them must be hopelessly lost ere long," persisted the French MS.; "whereas a *national* library forms a safe and abiding resting-place for books and MSS. I only wish I were safe and snug in some such refuge; who can tell into what common hands or dingy hole I may next fall. Now there is the Imperial Library of Paris! What a haven of refuge that has been for innumerable books and MSS., from the time of its foundation in the fourteenth century. Why, before a *printed* book was dreamt of, it possessed 1,000 volumes—MSS., of course. Then copies of the first printed books were taken to this haven, and there remained safe and cherished. What treasures must be there accumulated! Hundreds of thousands that perhaps can be met with nowhere else. The world certainly owes a great deal to the founder or founders of a *national* library, as our venerable friend the Folio remarked —men who have bequeathed to their country the treasured volumes which they have spent time, and labour, and money, and almost life itself in collecting."

"Yes, that is true indeed," said the Spenser, "such men deserve public honours; Cardinal Borromeo, for example, who, by bequeathing his collection of 40,000 volumes, formed the 'Ambrosian Library' at Milan; and the somewhat obscure, but studious, book-loving Nicholas Nicoli, who left his library to the public from love to his country. Poor man, his good intentions would not have been carried out, I believe, had it not been for the magnificent Cosmo de Medici;

for Nicoli died so deeply in debt, that his books would all have been sold to greedy creditors. But Cosmo took care that Nicoli's wishes were fulfilled. Cosmo also greatly enriched this same Florentine library with stores of Classic MSS., which he caused to be collected for him from far and near."

"While we are on Italian ground," said the Virgil, "allow me to remind you of the illustrious Cicero, who was so great a lover of everything belonging to literature, and who told his friend Atticus *not to spare his* (Cicero's) *purse,* but to collect for him everything he possibly could. Many were the choice and rare MSS. that Atticus sent to his friend's villa at Tusculum, and of which, if report speaks truly, he also managed to keep copies for himself. Then there was the rich and magnificent Lucullus, who so generously opened his splendid library to all the learned. Glorious days of delight those must have been, when books were honoured as they deserved, and treated as if they were almost sacred ; when the rooms in which they were preserved had marble floors, glass and ivory on their walls, and the desks on which the treasures stood were of cedar and ebony. Our Emperors were many of them men of letters as well as arms, and when they conquered, they did not destroy after the manner of barbarians, but preserved with care and reverence the literary treasures they found."

"Yes, and brought them away to their own country," remarked the Esop, *sotto voce.*

"Our own English libraries are in like manner indebted for their origin to the patriotic benevolence of private individuals. The reading-room of the British Museum, I have heard, commenced with a gift of 50,000 volumes from Sir Hans Sloane ; and our famous Bodleian Library at Oxford started with a collection that is said to have cost Sir Thomas Bodley £10,000. All honour be to such men," said the Great Folio.

"Pray, do not forget the noble Bishop Richard de Bury, Chancellor of England about 1341," said the English MS. "For he not only loved books for their own sake, but he spent time, and money, and labour in collecting them, for the express purpose that he might help students whose love might be as great, but whose purse was not as long, as his own. So wherever this good bishop, of blessed memory, travelled, he employed people to hunt up and collect all the literary treasures they could; especially the wandering friars, who, as they went about from place to place, had capital opportunities for hunting in out-of-the-way holes and corners. The bishop seems to have kept open house wherever he went, for he says that 'all of either sex, of any degree, estate, or dignity, whose pursuits were in any way connected with books, could with a knock most easily open the door of our heart.' "

" No wonder he was able to gather together a great number of treasures; but what did he do with them when he had made his collection?" asked the New Book.

" He established a library with them for Durham College, which was afterwards swallowed up into Trinity of Oxford, and in later times became almost entirely dispersed," replied the English MS.

" What a grievous pity," said the Great Folio. " This good bishop, as well as the other celebrated lovers of books who have been mentioned, must have felt their work to be ' *Labor absque labore*' (' The labour void of labour '), which motto stands, I have heard, as the inscription over the Florentine Library; and they acted in the spirit of another motto, the one at the Petersburg Library— '*Paulatim*' (' Little by little) '—as day by day they added first one treasure and then another to that which they considered ' more precious than rubies.' "

" What a tremendous number of books must have been written since the time when the *first prose* book was written," said the English MS. " It was in the century in which I was myself born that that first prose book was produced by Sir John Mandeville. I dare say you all remember that he was a great traveller. He went abroad about the year 1322, and this book was a description of his travels in the East. Sir John wrote it in 1356, first in Latin, but afterwards, as he tells us, he ' put this boke out of Latyn into Frenshe, and translated it again out of Frenshe into Englyssche, that every man of my nacioun may understand it.' Dear me; what a popular book it was to be sure. Wynken de Worde printed the first English edition of it at Westminster in 1499. Then in this fourteenth century the first really long English *poem* was published, if I may use the word for what was, of course, only a written book. I mean ' The Vision of Piers Ploughman,' written, I believe, by one Langlande."

" But there is an Anglo-Saxon poem, of much older date, by one who is called the Father of Anglo-Saxon poetry, and even the Anglo-Saxon Milton, because he, like Milton, sings of ' Paradise Lost,' " said the Great Folio.

" Yes ; you refer to Brother Cædmon, a native of Northumberland, and a monk of Whitby. The good monk wrote as he felt and thought, and made use of the terms common in his day. He speaks of Abraham as a mighty earl, a wise-heedy man ; and of the sons of Reuben as ' Vikings,' or sea-pirates. But I have heard that the oldest epic poem in any modern language, is one called ' Beowulf,' which is said to have been brought from Sleswick to England as early as the fifth century," replied the English MS.

" Pray, who was ' Beowulf,' or, rather, what was the poem about? I am ashamed to say I know nothing of it," said the New Book.

" No shame at all, my young friend," replied the Great Folio. " For the study of Anglo-Saxon literature is not so much attended to as it ought to be. It attracted little or no notice till the sixteenth century. Being myself in that century both young and ignorant, I know I used to wonder at people for caring anything at all about mere MSS., when there were *printed* books to be obtained, *vide* myself. Of course, I became wiser as I grew older. I remember that when this same poem ' Beowulf ' was first translated at Copenhagen, 1815, my then owner, an exceedingly learned man, was greatly delighted. But our friend will kindly describe the poem to you, I have no doubt."

" I know but little concerning it, and that little is all derived from hearsay," replied the English MS.; " but this is what I have heard :—' That somewhere in the fens of Jutland, in very early days (history does not say exactly when nor where), there lived a grim giant. This giant used to pay visits—uninvited visits—to the palace of a king named Hrothgar, just to see " how the Danes found themselves after their ale carouse," and on one of these pleasant little visits he killed thirty people, and ever after that the whole land was kept in fear of death. So a brave man named " Beowulf," the brother of King Hrothgar, determined to kill the giant. He came with fifteen brave men, fought the giant, tore off one of his arms, and hung it up on the palace walls. Retiring to his cave, the grim giant died, and thereupon was great rejoicing. Beowulf, the hero, did other wonderful things, which are told in this poem.' "

" Thank you," said the New Book. " Your account makes me wish to know more. I should think our later poets must be indebted greatly to these romances and poems of early days."

" Indeed, you may well say so," replied the Great Folio ; " Chaucer, Spenser, Shakespeare, and your own Tennyson, have drawn inspiration from the Anglo-Saxon and Welsh romances, and from the poetry of trouvères and troubadours, the northern and southern minstrels of sunny France. Thanks to such men as Geoffrey of Monmouth, and others, who collected and translated them. And where would modern history books be had it not been for the old Saxon and other chroniclers, such as Bede, William of Malmesbury, Henry of Huntingdon, Matthew Paris, and others, who with patience and care wrote the chronicles of the times in which they lived. It was well for the world that in those days there was a class of men set apart and devoted to peaceful pursuits, for they were the only ones who could wield the pen."

" Do not forget Anna Comnena, the daughter of Alexius I., who wrote the history of her father's reign in the beginning of the twelfth century ; nor my merry old countryman Frossart, who tells us, in his ' Chronicle,' what France, and Spain, and England were doing in the fourteenth century. Indeed, people can form little idea of the debt they owe to these old chroniclers, nor of the immense stores of information laid up in accumulated masses of MSS. Too many, even of those who profess to be ' historians,' and who ought therefore most thankfully to avail themselves of the aid we MSS. can afford, are apt to look upon us as *paperasses*—paper rubbish. Just as a certain Père Daniel, who undertook to write a history of France, described the 1,400 folios of MS. treasures which the king's librarian showed him, and which he ought to have been but too thankful to investigate. But no ; Père Daniel would not have the aid of any ' paper rubbish.' So he wrote his history after his own plan, and it is said that there are 10,000 blunders in it. So much for the wisdom of the historian who disdains the help to be derived from MSS."

" Still it must be confessed," said the English MS., " that valuable as we

MSS. confessedly are in all matters which relate to the past, yet that it was a very good thing for the world that the art of printing was invented just as soon as it was, for no number of good monks, however industrious, and no pens, however swift, could have kept pace with that desire for knowledge which seems to have come over mankind soon after that memorable era ; much less could they supply the call for 'news' and yet more 'news,' books and yet more books, which, judging from what our young friend has told us, appears to be ever and ever increasing."

"Well may you say so," exclaimed the New Book. "It would be quite impossible to give you any idea of the amount actually printed in any one single day, even in England, little island that it is ; much less throughout the civilised world. You remember what I said, when we were talking about the 'Newspaper Press,' as to the number of printed sheets that were turned off daily ; and I took but two newspapers, the *Times* and the *Scotsman*, as illustrations. But when you consider the number of different papers circulated in London, and that every town throughout England—and I may say the whole of Europe and America—of any size to speak of, has its own local paper, and very many towns have their three, four, or even more local papers, the number becomes overwhelming. Then add the number of weekly and monthly magazines in constant circulation ; add again the number of volumes, books, that are continually 'issuing from the press' at every one of the many printing establishments of this country, and I feel sure we should all give up the attempt to reckon the figures in absolute despair.

"To give you just a faint glimmer of a perception of the overwhelming number, I may perhaps mention that in 'Our Firm' we 'turn off' about 125,000 printed sheets a day ; or say, 12,500 volumes of ten sheets each. Now, if we take 300 working days to the year, that will give 3,750,000 volumes a year from our single firm."

"Dear me ; the number seems to be quite past belief, or would be so unless our authority was as good as we know it to be," said the English MS. "And I suppose most of these, or at least very many of these volumes will have passed through all the several processes you have so well described, and have employed as many different persons in the course of their passage 'through the press' as you have mentioned?"

"Yes, undoubtedly so, more or less," replied the New Book. "And the number of persons employed in every large firm which combines in itself all or most of the various branches of 'book-producing' is something considerable. For instance, there is a firm at Strasburg which employs upwards of 200; one at Vienna employing upwards of 300; one at Leipzig upwards of 400; while at the establishment of M. Mame, of Tours, there are more than 1,000."

"And how many people are employed at the establishment from whence you came?" asked the Esop.

"Well, we have not room to do all our work under one roof, as we combine all the different branches; but we employ in our London premises more than 500 persons about what may be called, for the sake of distinction, the *manual* part of the production of books, such as the printing, binding, engraving, publishing; while taking the higher and the lower departments of labour together, those which relate to the *minds* as well as the *bodies* of books, I believe you would find the number of persons employed to be between 700 and 800," replied the New Book.

"It takes so much time and labour, so much skill and thought, to produce a printed book, that it seems to me a very great pity that any but thoroughly good and sensible books should be passed through the press," said the Quarto.

"Ah, perhaps you would recommend that we should go back to those good old days when there were 'licensers for the press,' who not only declared whether a book should or should not be printed, but who also took upon themselves the right to cut out any passage that might not please them," said the Law Book.

"Or perhaps our friend would prefer to have the 'Index Expurgatorius' in force; especially the 'simple index' which contains a list of condemned books 'never to be opened,'" said the Elzevir.

"If that were to be so," said the Esop, "our friend the Quarto might find himself on the list, and others of us in this room would, I suspect, share a similar fate."

"These 'licensers for the press' were in England first formally established in the reign of King Charles I.," remarked the Great Folio. "How indignant the great Milton was about it. 'These executioners of books,' as he calls them, and grandly and nobly did he plead for and defend the right of a *free press.*"

"And so it did become in 1694," said the Law Book, "and I suppose is so at this present day."

"Yes, happily we have no set of persons licensed to draw their pen through this and the other phrase, or alter a passage to suit their own ideas. I should imagine nothing could well be more annoying to an author than to have things put down to him which he never meant to say, and things left out which he wished to say. But at the present day authors may write pretty much what they like (except, perhaps, the editors of papers, who are unlucky enough sometimes to get into scrapes); and any one (if he can pay for it) may print any amount of trash he likes. The great comfort is, that no one is obliged to read it, if he does not wish."

"The people of these days must be very great readers, since so many books are yearly published; I wonder if they would like to have a certain old bishop's scheme of education carried out, which was, that there should be a 100 *folio* volumes written, on the most important branches of knowledge, and that the *Government should compel* its subjects to read them," said the English MS.

"The poor subjects!" exclaimed the New Book. "Such a scheme would be sufficient to overturn any Government of the present day, the Opposition benches would be so crowded; for though our young people certainly can and do read an immense number of volumes in a short space of time, yet the reading is of the kind that is 'light' but *not* 'nutritious.' A 100 *folios*, bah! they would die of disgust before they were through the first."

"Still I maintain my former proposition," said the Quarto drily, "that it is a grievous waste to bestow so much care, and thought, and time, and skill, on the printing and publishing of bad or foolish books; it is worse, far worse than waste."

"Then you do not agree with the elder Pliny, that there is no book so bad, but that we may get some profit of it?" said the Virgil.

"Certainly not," replied the Quarto, stiffly.

"As to really *bad* books, I have nothing to say on their behalf. But as to the books often pronounced to be 'stupid' or 'dry,' I think something might be urged in mitigation of the sweeping sentence passed on them by the respected Quarto,' said the New Book. "It must be remembered that almost every book, be it stupid or clever, brilliant or dull, has, at some time or other, had some one person specially interested in it; some one to whom it belonged in a particular manner, as a child to the parent; some one who had a tender compassion for its defects, a pleasant pride in its excellences, a fellow-feeling in its failure, a supreme satisfaction in its success. We know how our authors regarded *us*—how dear we were to them—how they lived in us, and by us, and for us—how impossible it was to them to separate themselves from us. For the sake of the one person interested in the fate of each individual book, let us be tolerant even of the stupid ones."

"I am sure we can all confirm what our young friend has just said, as to the close relationship that exists between an author and the book or books which he has himself written," said the Great Folio. "And as we remain in this world long after the brain that conceived us, and the fingers that penned us, have passed away, we serve to prolong the life, and perpetuate the name, and extend the fame of the author to whom we owe our existence. Well might the great Milton exclaim that 'a good book is the precious life-blood of a master-spirit, embalmed and treasured up on purpose to a life beyond life.'"

Much applause followed these remarks. When quiet was restored, the Great Folio resumed: "It is now my pleasant duty to express, in the name of this society, the great satisfaction we have experienced in listening to our young friend's able and interesting account of the way in which he 'passed through the press.' By it, he has not only enabled us to revive our recollections of a similar passage in our own lives, long years ago, but he has given to us a great deal of information as to the ways and doings of the world in the present day. I beg him, therefore, to accept the thanks of this society."

"I can only say," replied the New Book, in acknowledging this vote of thanks, "that I am exceedingly obliged by the kind way in which all the members of this society have listened to my history; and if I have been able in any degree to add to their already large stores of knowledge, I am quite sure that my own small stock has been increased by their valuable and interesting remarks. And now I have only to add in confidence that I am published by Messrs. CASSELL, PETTER, and GALPIN, La Belle Sauvage Yard, Ludgate Hill."

A general shutting up then followed, after which perfect silence settled on the room.

AGAIN a dark, dreary afternoon, and again the same old gentleman was to be seen in the same dusty, dingy room. But this time he was not alone; with him was a bright, restless boy of seven years of age.

"O, grandpapa! do come away from this ugly place," exclaimed the child, after he had been a very few minutes in the room. "You said you would buy me something pretty, and I'm quite certain there's nothing pretty here. Do let us go."

The child was flitting about from one part of the room to another while speaking, unable to keep still for a moment. All at once his eye caught sight of our "New Book."

"Oh! but here is a beautiful book!" exclaimed the boy; "and see, *such a lot* of pictures! Oh, grandpapa, please—please buy me this."

"Why, I do declare," said the old gentleman, taking the book out of the child's hands, "this is the very 'Robinson Crusoe' I bought for you the other day, and thought I must have lost it in the omnibus."

"This for *me*—my very *own*. Why, it really *is* ' Robinson ;' see, here he is in his real skin coat. You are a jolly good grandpapa. Let us make haste home to show it to mamma."

And pulling his grandpapa by the coat, the happy, impatient child hurried him out of the room, carrying away with him, tucked under his little arm, our young friend " the New Book."